LUNCH
WITH MARIA

MARIA ORLANDO
& NICK PAPPAS

ISBN (Paperback): 978-0-9983007-4-0

ISBN (Ebook): 978-0-9983007-5-7

Book design by Nuno Moreira, NM DESIGN

PROMETHEUS
BOOKS, LLC.
...the fire remains

LUNCH
WITH MARIA

A SICILIAN ODYSSEY

MARIA ORLANDO
& NICK PAPPAS

PREFACE

everything happens for a reason -
there are no coincidences

PROLOGUE

Everyone is familiar with the story of Helen of Troy – the face that launched a thousand ships. Homer wrote about her in the *Iliad* and the *Odyssey*, and Virgil did as well in *The Aeneid*. Good stuff.

But the real story is that it was actually a Jersey Girl who saved not only history, but also, a history teacher is less well known.

CHAPTER ONE
BACK IN SCHOOL

A SUBURBAN NEW JERSEY HIGH SCHOOL – 2019

"Hey, man, what duty do you have? Another no-show piece of cake?"

"Hi to you, too, knucklehead. How was your summer?"

The above two public speaking geniuses were teachers at Brighton High School, an excellent school in an affluent area of New Jersey. The day before the kids would arrive for the first day of classes. The two were going through all the paperwork that was part of staff preparation. They were good friends and pretty fair teachers, but they liked to bust each other every chance they got.

"I think I have lunch duty again."

"What did you do to deserve that? They must hate you. That's ten years in a row, isn't it?"

"Something like that. But actually, I asked for it."

"Are you crazy?"

"It's not bad, and the cafeteria is close to my room. Of course, a lot depends on who your partner is. The last couple of years, it's been good – nice ladies and nice-looking, too."

"Who's with you this year?

"Don't know. I haven't checked yet. I hope it's someone I get along with."

"Well, since ninety percent of the staff hates your guts, there's not much chance of that, is there?"

"OK, crap head. You know it's only about eighty percent. Who cares, anyway?"

Their trip to math land was interrupted by an announcement. "Staff. Anyone who has lunch duty, please meet with Mr. Jenkins in his office in fifteen minutes."

"Well, I guess I'll find out in a couple. Why we have to have a meeting is beyond me. Everyone has done this before, right, Jim? So, what's the point?"

"Stop whining, Nick. Most things are beyond you. You know that. And he probably doesn't even know why he has it. Maybe so that he could say he had it. Who the hell knows? Do you want me to take your stuff down to your room?"

"Yeah, would you? Thanks, man. Catch you later."

"Good luck with your partner tomorrow!"

CHAPTER TWO
THE SICILIAN

The next day was the first "real" day of school - in other words, all the kids were in class. Nick had just taught three classes and had two more coming up, and he was mentally gassed. Now he had to deal with being on lunch duty. He prayed that the students would be at least reasonably good while they were eating because he was not in the mood for confrontation. Where was the other teacher?

"Hello, hello."

He was just getting settled in his chair when he heard what would become a daily salutation from his lunch duty partner, whom he overlooked walking in. Her arms were loaded with books of all sorts.

"Holy shit," he exclaimed to himself as he turned to face her. Only it wasn't to himself; anyone within twenty feet could hear him. He couldn't have known it at the time, but these would be both the first words and the last words he would utter in the cafeteria this year...Strike one--

"I beg your pardon?"

"Oh, I'm sorry. I banged my knee, and I didn't mean to say that."

The hell he didn't. He didn't mean to say it out loud, but if you had been there and were a "regular guy," believe me, you would have said the same thing. His lunch duty partner was Maria Orlando, an English teacher. To say she was striking would be the mother of all understatements. Maria was about five-three, dark hair, sultry and provocative, with the most beautiful eyes he had ever seen. She was Sicilian, and if you can find a better-looking group of women anywhere on earth, please let me know where that might be. As for Nick, after the initial expletive and apology, he was speechless. But he kept repeating his initial outburst to himself-- repeatedly--"holy shit, holy shit, holy shit." Maria looked at him as if he had two heads, for he sat there just staring at her, and no other words appeared to be forthcoming any time soon. Moments like this would be the first of many holes he would dig for himself over the school year. Strike two--

"Nick, are you OK?"

Wow, she knew his name. Well, of course, she did. They had been teaching in the same building for the past fifteen years and would say "Hi" casually whenever they ran into each other - or sometimes even "Yiasou," since Nick was Greek. (She spoke Greek as well as he did). But this was the closest he had ever been to her--holy shit!

He finally managed to blurt out another lame comment.

"Yeah, I'm fine. I didn't know you would be my partner, and I was just taken by surprise, that's all."

"Well, Nick, I hope you're not disappointed!" He almost choked on the coffee he had been drinking.

"I wasn't at the meeting in Jenkins' office, but my name is on the sheet, isn't it?"

Nick had no good answer in what would become a too often repeated situation as the days went on. The truth was that he had seen her name on the list but just brushed it off. He didn't recall that she was so goddamn good-looking, especially when she was sitting in the chair next to him - literally an arm's length away. But instead of just saying that he must have missed her name, or that he misread it, or didn't have his glasses...or that he was just a stupid asshole, he told the truth. This became another "disturbing" pattern in their relationship: he found it impossible to lie to her—what a dope.

"Well, to tell you the truth, Maria, now that I think of it, I did see your name, but I uh, well…"

"Figured it wasn't worth a second glance, huh?" She was laughing as she said this, which made her even more alluring, if that were even possible. He was pretty sure she wasn't laughing *with* him.

Strike three, holy shit….

CHAPTER THREE
ANOTHER DISTURBING
PRECEDENT

He didn't realize it, but he was setting up a template for his day that would stay with him all year and cause him scores of worries and second guesses. At the same time, it would bring some of the most satisfying moments of his life. He probably should have been able to figure it out, and many people would surely have seen what was coming beforehand. But he was not a lot of people - he was Nick Pappas, a rock-headed, worrisome, emotional, and insecure Greek, and he was about to embark on an odyssey that would make Odysseus' ten-year journey seem like a walk in the park. Be that as it may, his immediate problem was to get to his next class, and while it was less than a hundred feet from the cafeteria to his room, he had to navigate through what seemed like every student in New Jersey. He hated to be late on the first day, so he gave his elbows free rein as he blistered through the mob, taking out two freshmen, a garbage can, and his buddy from across the hall.

"Hey, Jim, sorry, man. I was just trying to get to class." He helped pick up his friend, who was laughing uncontrollably at what had just happened.

"Are you all right?"

Jim was dusting himself off but was still in the middle of a big belly laugh. "I'm fine. It's just that in twenty years here, I've never seen you move so fast. Were you running 'to' or 'from'?"

Nick's class was just getting there in groups of two or three, and he pointed to the door to indicate he wanted them to go in.

"Hey, Mr. Pappas, you got me again," cracked a massive-looking student, who had essentially followed the teacher down from the cafeteria. "I can't wait," he grinned as he high fived his teacher.

"Yeah, Tommy, me, too," Nick deadpanned while shaking his head.

"P.I.A.,?" Jim inquired.

"Well, he's OK...but there are moments—"

"Yeah, I know the type," Jim replied. "So, you never told me why you were in such a damn hurry. Was Brad on your tail?"

Brad was the principal. Not a bad guy, as principals go, but he could be a real pain with his anal, everything exactly "just so" attitude.

"No, I haven't even seen him today - thankfully. I just didn't want to be late. That's all."

"Well, you got about a minute. You're good. Where were you coming from?"

"Lunch duty."

"Hey, you snake, you never told me who your partner was."

"Maria. Maria Orlando."

"Whoa, be careful, buddy. Nice to look at but watch out."

Nick was about to ask him what he meant when the bell rang. Another class to break in. "Watch out? Watch out for what?" he kept wondering as he tried to focus on history.

CHAPTER FOUR
YOU CAN'T THINK AND
TEACH AT THE SAME TIME

Now Nick was a huge baseball fan, and he often used sports metaphors during class discussions. Sometimes, he would even base a test question on some ballplayer, situation, or quote. Hardly a test went by where there wasn't some reference to the sports world. If you were a baseball player, famous or infamous, you probably found your way onto an assignment or test, and if you uttered some relevant phrase or other -- bingo, it was fodder for Pappas! He had one of his all-time favorite sayings painted on his wall over the whiteboard: "THROW THE BALL HARD" - Tony Lupien, Dartmouth Baseball. Of course, Yogi Berra was a goldmine for quotes, and one of his favorites was "You can't think and hit at the same time." Well, the same goes for teaching. You have to "think," but you have to be in the flow of what is happening, or the kids will be about two miles ahead of you. Unfortunately, he was not only thinking but obsessing about a petite brunette whose image he couldn't shake if he wanted to. How the hell was he supposed to teach? Of course, this was the first day of school, when you needed to be especially on your game to set the tone for the rest of the year. He always tried to do something different, out of the ordinary, to kick things off, but as he walked to the front of the room, not only couldn't he think of what he had planned to do, he couldn't remember what class it was that he was facing. He looked over at Tommy, the big kid who had high-fived him. What the hell year was he? That might give him a clue.

"Hey Tom," he called out with his best bluster. "What class did you have me for?"

"Homeroom. Last year. Don't you remember?" Some quick mental arithmetic later, and he had the answer; since Nick had only Freshmen homerooms, and he had him last year, it could only mean that Tommy was a sophomore and that this had to be US History. Whew. All this took about a millisecond, and it all came back to him. He could still see Maria's face, but at least he had a sense of what he was gonna do.

"OK, people, close your eyes, put your heads down, and think. That's right, just relax…."

"Hey, Mr. Pappas, you got any pillows," one of his new charges called out.

"When you're a senior. Sophomores get a hard desk," he jokingly responded.

The teacher quietly placed a marker and piece of computer paper on the desk of each student; of course, he could have had them out before the class had started, but it was a little game he played with himself to see if he could do it without disturbing any of them. Plus, he had forgotten all about it. Well, no harm, no foul. "Good job, Nick," he whispered under his breath. Why couldn't he have been this quiet during the beginning of lunch? Well, he figured he'd better get going. He was at the top of the salary guide, and they would love to get rid of him and save some money. The last thing he needed was some administrator walking by and seeing him musing about his botched first impression with his lunch duty compatriot.

Nick had a bat in his room and often in his hand, which he would sometimes use as part of his lesson or to get the class's attention. It was an old wooden one, a Mickey Mantle model, still in good shape but with a lot of batting practice marks on it. He usually had it when he stood in the hall between classes, and it would scare the crap out of the freshmen who were scurrying by trying to find their way. Today it would serve as a great alarm clock. He slammed it on an empty desk in front of the room, eliciting some yelps, screams, and laughs. Some of them already knew Nick from just talking to him or from one of their older siblings, and they took the crack of the bat pretty much in stride. Many of the others had a bewildered look, which was just what he wanted.

"OK, you should have on your desk a piece of paper and a marker, and I know it's the first day of school, but you need about 87% of your brain to complete the following thinking exercise." The percentage of your brain needed on that particular day or for that assignment was another one of his trademarks. It let the class know if it was something they could coast through (around 70% or so) or if they had to get their brains in gear (85% and above). And - it was fun!

"On one side of the paper, draw...yes draw...what was going through your mind while you had your heads down. Anything - but draw it, and be ready to explain what you drew and why you chose that particular thing to illustrate. On the other side, draw and label something that you think symbolizes the USA today - and, yeah, be ready to talk about it a bit....! Got it? Any questions?"

A hand went up in the left corner of the room. "I have a quick question."

"Sure," Pappas replied. "What's your name?"

"Diane. Uh, are you looking for something in particular?"

"Good question. I am looking for you to think. Understand?"

She said she did, and there were no other questions, which meant either they got it or were content just to wing it and see what happened.

"Good. Seventeen minutes give or take. Put your marker down to let me know when you're done."

Pappas rarely, if ever, gave a round number in which his classroom activities had to be completed. He reasoned that it made people ponder things if the time limit were "different." A lot of people thought Pappas was "different," but he was fine with that.

The class worked quietly, which allowed him to go over what he would do with the juniors coming in next period. Of course, it was hard to get his mind away from Maria, but he could not have possibly realized the scope or breath of the adventure that he was about to undertake. How could he??

EMAIL BREAK........ A TALK WITH AN OLD FRIEND

To: npappas
Fr: dlayten
Re: first day

Hey man, how was your first day of school? The people running baseball are idiots. They should put us in charge. Yeah. Ha Ha. Who did you get for your lunch duty partner? I hope it was some switch-hitter - that would give you something to complain about. Gimme a holler when you get a chance.

The "Babe"

To: dlayten
Fr: npappas
Re: HA!

Hey yourself. First day OK, as things go. Classes seem all right. A lot of the kids already think I am nuts, so I am a bit ahead of schedule. Got some shit to do...catch up with you tomorrow. By the way, lunch duty partner is an English teacher named Maria. She has eyes to die for.....!!

Jeter

The two best friends had known each other since high school and had stayed close ever since. They each had done a tour in Vietnam, Nick as an Army artillery officer, Doug on a Navy destroyer. Over the years, they had countless sessions of batting practice, dozens of stickball games and trips to batting cages, weekly hoops at the "Y," probably forty or so Yankees games, and literally hundreds of hours just driving around and shooting the breeze. They were like brothers, and even though distance had made getting together rare, they emailed each other at least two- or three-times a a week, always signing the emails as someone else - either a celebrity or someone they had known from back in the day. (Neither one of them knew how that got started, but it had been going on for more decades than they would admit.) They always said what they believed in these "Virtual" conversations, yet many of their remarks were facetious and tongue in cheek. You had to know these guys to figure out what they really meant, and that's just how they liked it. Oh, there was a quick response to Nick's email:

To: npappas

Fr: dlayten

Re: "EYES TO DIE FOR"

You lucky bastard!!

Jimmy Stewart

CHAPTER FIVE
"DEJA VU, ALL OVER AGAIN"

Nick looked at the clock: 5:30. Well, it was really five o'clock. He kept the alarm thirty minutes fast to be sure he would be on time for things. So, should he get up and be tired for the day but at least get to school on time, or should he roll over and get another half hour or so of sleep. Of course, he would risk not getting up on time, being late for the day, and still being tired. It was a lose, lose situation, so he dragged his butt out of bed and turned on the coffee. Nick was the antithesis of a morning person. He barely knew who he was before his daily dose of java, and it was a good five minutes before Nick realized that he had forgotten to set up the coffee the night before, so he threw some water and coffee into the pot and hoped for the best.

Nick rarely measured the ingredients anyway, but today he was winging it —well, really "flinging" it! He rummaged through the cabinets till he uncovered the other half of a corn muffin he had started the day before, grabbed the pot before it was quite finished, and managed to get some in the cup and on his hand. Luckily, no one was around to hear the string of expletives pouring out of his mouth. He finally settled with his muffin and his coffee - which was good - amazingly enough - and set out to assess the state of things. The second day of school was usually a bit easier than the first. However, the schedule was still out of whack to accommodate class meetings and other "necessary" prerequisites for the new year. His mind wandered a bit back to his first day of high school as a student, which was like every other day except for the anticipation and just a slight case of nerves. There were no orientations, coddling, or handholding; it was sink or swim, and he felt better. Everything older seemed better.

He poured another half a cup and got his mind back to the present. His classes seemed to have gone fairly well, although he really couldn't remember any of them except the one right after lunch duty. Well, he chalked his vague memory to the time of day. And after twenty years of teaching, he should have it pretty well figured out, and if he couldn't remember every detail, who would know, and anyway, who cares. One thing was pretty certain: about half the kids were afraid of him, and the rest thought he was crazy. Pretty much a perfect ratio, although some students were in both categories. He still had some nerves opening up a new year, but he seemed to have had them under control when he returned yesterday. One thing he did remember was lunch duty. "What a fool Maria must think I am," he thought to himself as he watched the sun peeking through the blinds. He resolved to apologize profusely and sincerely and never to make an ass of himself like that again. He didn't know it at the time, but he would succeed in his first endeavor--time and time again. But making an ass of himself would become as much a part of his day as having his morning jolt of caffeine.

He threw on a CD to keep him company while he showered and shaved. He often did his best creative thinking in the bathroom, but he decided to take a morning off from anything related to the curriculum and figure out what he would say at lunchtime. Should he start with a casual hello and then get into it, blame it on first-day missteps, or just play it by ear? One thing was for sure: he wanted to stay on the good side of Maria, whom he knew only casually, but who, besides being very easy on the eyes, was a tough person to deal with, and he didn't want to get on her bad side. Or, more accurately, even deeper on her bad side. He stepped out of the shower and almost broke his neck on a tube of toothpaste that had no business being on the floor. Well, no one to blame but himself. As he started shaving, an uneasy feeling, which had been permeating his whole adventure in the bathroom, seemed to become more pronounced and foreboding. He couldn't figure it out, but he knew something wasn't quite the way it should be. Well, it would probably come to him; he just had to tell himself that he would think of it sooner or later, and ninety percent of the time, it would pop up. It was a good technique and saved him a lot of worrying. Lord knows, he had enough problems without making this into another one.

Well, he'd better get going. The first day of school was on Thursday, making today the second day, Friday. Wow, those math teachers have a lot to deal with, don't they? He chuckled as he threw on some deodorant and aftershave. He wondered if "dress-down Fridays" were supposed to start right away, but since he felt like wearing jeans, and he didn't care all that much if it were "official" yet, he thought he might as well set a precedent. So, he threw on a dark green pullover shirt and a pair of dark blue coach's pants. Comfortable and, as he passed the mirror, not particularly bad if he did say so himself.

He grabbed his briefcase and threw it in the back seat of his Chevy. Hmmm, when was the lease up on this car? Well, it wasn't today, hopefully. He turned on the radio started the twenty-minute drive to the high school, which was, in his estimation, the nicest commute of anyone in the state. The road wound its way over a picturesque mountain, complete with a stream, herds of sheep, and a little shed that was the home of two of the cutest donkeys he had ever seen.

The DJ was talking about a dream he had the night before—Dream!! That was it!! Nick slammed the steering wheel and almost went off the small bridge he was crossing. "Dream! I didn't have my nightmare this year!" he yelled so loud that one of the donkeys turned his head to see who this madman might be. Just about every year, a few days before going back to teach, Nick would have what he called his "nightmare" about school. While the details were usually different, its gist was always the same: he would be in school in front of the class and be unprepared, embarrassed, acting stupid, or all of the above. Sometimes he couldn't find his plans; other times, the kids wouldn't pay attention. Often, he was in his underwear. But he didn't remember having it this year. He was proud of himself for figuring out what had been bothering him. He was good to go - or so he thought.

Nick pulled into the faculty parking lot. He was hoping to talk to Maria before she got into the school. Maria's room was on the floor above his, and if he missed her in the lot, he would probably have to wait till lunch to see her, and his behavior the day before was still gnawing at him. Her car was already there. Damn, he cursed under his breath. Okay, this would give him more time to work on his mea culpa speech. There were restrooms adjacent to the entrance, and, as luck would have it, Maria was just coming out of the ladies' room, loaded with books.

"Maria," he called out. "I just wanted to explain about yesterday."

The look on her face was bewilderment, and Nick felt as if he had just taken a step backward in his endeavor to apologize.

"Hey, can I catch up with you at lunchtime? I've got to get some stuff ready.

You know we have lunch duty together, right? See you then."

Confusion was nothing new to Nick. He had gone through the better part of his life not knowing what the hell was going on; at least, that's what he had been told many times, both by others and by his inner voice. But this was a new low. Did she think he couldn't remember from one day to the next? What was she talking about? And there was another thing: she was dressed to the nines, which would make for some nice staring on his part come lunchtime, but Maria loved to dress down as well (and she looked just as good in jeans as she did in a dress). Why was she dressed up?

His reverie was interrupted by the first announcement of the day.

"Good morning, everyone. Welcome back to another school year. Remember that you are to report to your homerooms before starting your regular classes. Thank you and have a good day and a good year."

God, did Nick hate the announcements, especially redundant ones. Why the hell were they welcoming everyone back "again"? Well, at least they were consistent: it was an unnecessary and annoying interruption. And he knew this was just the beginning. There were at least thirty announcements a day, and after all these years at the school, he knew he shouldn't let it bother him. But Nick was Nick, and he also knew that no matter how hard he tried, these "messages" would annoy him, though, to be honest, he didn't try at all. Today, he had other things on his mind, foremost of which was smoothing things out with a feisty Sicilian. He had arrived before most of the faculty and, more importantly, most of the students. This would give him a chance to get things under control.

For a disorganized person, Nick did have some things that had become Pavlovian as he made his way to his classroom. He always said something nasty to Dave Chapman, a young teacher whom Nick liked. Dave was easy pickings for some good-natured barbs to start the day. Then he'd throw on a CD or a record (Oldies was the choice this morning), make the coffee, and pop across the hall to talk some baseball with Jim, his best friend on the staff.

He was singing along to one of the Do Wop groups as the coffee was perking and took out some of the things he would need from his briefcase. A cardboard box sat on the floor near his desk, filled with the appointment calendars the homeroom teachers gave out to the kids. He had done that yesterday. Why was he getting some more? Well, they had probably been delivered to the wrong room, so he grabbed a hot cup of coffee and went across the hall to kid Jim about the game the Cubs had blown the night before.

He found his friend putting a calendar on each desk in his room, to his surprise. "What are you doing, man?" Nick asked incredulously.

"Hey, Nick. I just like to have everything on their desks when they come in. I know you just give'em out right from the box, but it's a bit less confusing this way."

"Confusing" had suddenly become the key word in Nick's vocabulary.

"You mean we have another set of books to give out?"

Before Jim could answer, his cell phone went off. He pointed to it, indicating it was a call he had to take. Nick just nodded in understanding and pointed to his friend with one finger, an old sign they had developed between them indicating "catch you later."

Nick went back to his room, got some more coffee, and sat down at his desk. Something wasn't making sense. Nothing was making any sense. He flipped on his computer and glanced down at the day and date: "THURSDAY, SEPTEMBER 5." Thursday? That was yesterday, wasn't it? His mouth dropped three-quarters of the way to the floor as It finally hit him - today was yesterday, and yesterday was today. But how was that possible? What about all the stuff that happened at lunch duty yesterday and during his class the period after? Was he crazy? Or was he just--dreaming?? That had to be it. The nightmare! He had had it, after all. That was the only possible answer. He had thought that the first day of school had already taken place when it had all been just a dream. Could that happen in real life? As weird as it seemed, that was the only explanation plausible enough to make sense. Or, in reality, to come close to making sense. That's why the morning announcements were wishing everyone a good school year, why Jim was giving out books, and why Maria didn't know what he was talking about. Nick figured he'd just have to go with that explanation, as far out as it seemed. He had no idea that he was about to embark on an adventure that would make "the dream" seem like a cup of coffee.

Well, his first dilemma was what to tell Maria. He would have to come up with something that sounded semi-plausible and, at the same time, not too ridiculous. Well, he would have till lunchtime to figure something out.

He double-checked his email to see if anything else besides his sanity that he needed to take care of. Nope, nothing there that was pressing. The last message was from Doug: "You lucky bastard." He flipped on the sent messages, and there was the one where he told Doug about his first day. And about Maria. How the hell could he have told his friend about yesterday when there was no "yesterday," at least not yet. But hadn't he seen that--yesterday?? In his dream? Oh, God--what was happening?

CHAPTER SIX
1250 YEARS BC - GIVE OR TAKE

MOUNT OLYMPUS

Zeus was not having a good day. He had had too much wine the night before, and though he had intended to get a couple of important things done this morning, not only did his hangover preclude his getting to work on them, but he also couldn't remember what they were. On top of his splitting headache, his wife would surely be in one of her "I told you so" modes about the drinking. That's what he was dreading most of all--

"Bang," what sounded like a gunshot exploded in his ear. Of course, it would be many centuries before someone invented gunpowder, so it couldn't have been that. The king of the gods turned around to see his wife grinning from ear to ear. Her palms were a ruby shade of red, and, hungover as he was, he got it - it was one of her infamous "thunderclaps," which she produced by slamming her hands together with all the divine royal power she could muster.

"Well, oh mighty one, you are finally awake. I thought you were going to spend the day on your back. Oh, wait, that was pretty much your position last night, wasn't it!"

She let out a laugh that echoed through the heavens. It shook the heavens. The scowl on her husband's face was enough to stop the sun, but the more he grimaced and clutched his throbbing head, the louder and more piercing Hera's raucous behavior became.

"OK, say it. Just go ahead and say it," Zeus bellowed. "Say 'I told you so' and get it over with." He grabbed a pitcher and poured the contents on his head in a futile attempt to ease his present condition. Unfortunately, what he thought was water turned out to be hot coffee. He let out a scream that could still be heard in some parts of Greece. Of course, this set Hera off on another fit of laughter as she clutched her stomach and doubled over in glee.

Zeus was drying himself off and cursing - not in that order. Despite his misery, Hera's countenance was becoming infectious, and his agony notwithstanding, the king of the gods was starting to show just a glimmer of a smile.

"There's the man I love," Hera sighed as she patted her husband on the shoulder.

"The 'man'? Don't you mean the god?" Zeus retorted, tongue in cheek.

"Well, today, you were just a hungover guy. But you're still *my* guy. Just watch the volume of wine next time you throw one of your shindigs, OK?"

"Yeah, yeah. By the way, darling, what was that I just scalded myself with."

"It's called coffee. It's gonna be all the rage someday. I thought we'd try it. Did you like it?"

"Well, I have to admit, as it was scorching my face, I did happen to get a quick taste of it. Where did you get it?"

"Well, I was visiting my cousin yesterday at Delphi, and--"

"That's it," Zeus boomed. "DELPHI!"

"No, no need to go all the way down there--I will make more coffee. The Oracle gave me a huge bag of it. People in the future will drink it all the time. But we don't have to wait for that, do we! I'll put on a pot while you clean up."

"No, no, no. I just remembered that I need to find out something from the Oracle. Something big that's going to happen will change something that's supposed to happen unless we do something about it. Understand?"

"I'd better put on some coffee. It's supposed to help you sober up."

Zeus started to shake his head vehemently.

"No time."

Hera grabbed his wrist.

"Listen, dear, you may be a hotshot up here, but if you go see her looking like this and talking incoherently, she will throw you out. You know how finicky she can be!

And, speaking of time, this is her 'time' of the month, and she is a bit more testy than usual."

Zeus knew that his wife was right. Although he was ostensibly the ruler of heaven and earth, it was not a good idea to mess with someone who could see into the future and who also had, in the past, been very helpful to him in his job of taking care of the universe. Although she was wrong in her predictions quite often, at the very least, her "Visions" gave the big guy something to go on. She also had read him the riot act on several occasions, and he did not want to aggravate her today, so he agreed to clean up while his wife put on the "coffee."

"By the way, dear, what is this epic happening you have to take care of. And who told you about it?"

Zeus turned toward Hera and scratched the top of his head, which showed that he was not too clear about things.

"Well, I'm not sure exactly. Something about Sparta and Sicily and two beautiful women. That's about all he knew."

"He? He, who?" Hera wanted to know.

"Poseidon."

"Oh God, pardon my French," Hera exclaimed. "Why do you listen to anything he has to say? He's been in the depths so long his brain is waterlogged."

"I know, dear, but I can't take any chances. Poseidon is my younger brother, and he's bound to be right one of these times."

"OK. I guess there's a first for everything. Get dressed, get sober, stay calm."

"I wonder if mortals ever have days like this?" he whispered as he ducked behind a cloud to get himself ready.

CHAPTER SEVEN
DO YOU WANT TO KNOW
A SECRET?

Zeus made his way down off the mountain and took the mortal way to Delphi, which took him longer but also gave him a chance to think. His head was beginning to clear, and things were coming back to him, but that's not always a good thing when you are the top dog. Sometimes it's better when you're kind of foggy or don't have a clue at all. When you're lucid, you have no excuse, and you're the one that everyone - mortals and immortals alike - blames for just about everything. The other part of the equation was that this woman was insufferable. Just because she knew the future, or at least purported to know it, made her almost impossible to deal with, especially when her "visions" were necessary. Of course, she claimed all her visions were important, from the weather the next day to who would win at the Olympics. And then there was the political stuff, about which she was, in his opinion, an amateur posing as a pundit. But, he had to check this out just in case, so it was with a heavy heart and a slightly burned face that Zeus walked down the path to the Temple of Apollo.

One good thing was the setting, the Oracle notwithstanding. Delphi was nestled in a gorgeous valley, filled with olive trees intertwined with grape vines, framed by graceful and delicate cypress and chestnut trees. It was beautiful then and still is today. For all his bluster, Zeus appreciated beauty, whether it was a woman or the fading light shining through a radiant sunset, or the tranquility of a secluded grove in the heart of Greece. Preoccupied with the crisis in which he was about to be privy and immersed in the seclusion of the surroundings, Zeus wasn't paying attention to where he was walking. All at once, his head felt as if someone had stuck it to a hive. Which is exactly where it happened to be, as the almighty ruler had bumped into a low-slung branch of a tree and disturbed a settlement of what seemed like a thousand angry hornets. Telling them who he was did no good, and for some reason, his godlike powers never worked well here, hence the origin of the term "godforsaken place." But Zeus was in no mood for either word etymology or to try to find out why he was impotent at Delphi, which he swore he would figure out someday. But today, he had other things to deal with, the most immediate being these damn insects. Besides the apparent disturbance to their abode, the hornets were attracted to the residual smell of the coffee and the ointment Zeus had applied to ease the burns. He started to pull them off one by one, which was painstakingly slow. Then, wham, they changed their tactics. They kept buzzing around his head, but they stopped stinging. He was puzzled, but "don't look a gift hornet in its stinger," he thought. He couldn't help a bit of a smile at his witticism, but the gruesome sight soon wiped it out. He looked up to behold: it was Pythia, with her hands raised above her head and smiling ear to ear. Just what he needed: - a gloating oracle. Zeus figured his day could not possibly get any worse! But he was dead wrong....

CHAPTER EIGHT
ZEUS MEETS HIS MATCH

Pythia always considered Zeus to be somewhat of a dolt. Her insolence and condescending attitude rankled the head man wherever he even thought of her, and visiting her in her lair, as he called it, was worse than his requisite trips to the Underworld. And now, in the middle of the hornets and the pricker bushes, to hear her laughter resounding throughout the valley was almost more than he could bear. Had she been a mortal or even a low-level god, he would have turned her into a rock long ago. But unbeknownst to most of us living today, even the gods had restrictions, eternal rules they had to follow no matter what - or risk losing their elevated status. They were not allowed to kill indiscriminately, or even for a good reason, for that matter, unless it was in battle or to save a good person from an evil one. And, you didn't mess with "Fate" in any of its manifestations, the chief of which was "this damned woman," which was one of the nicer things Zeus called her.

He was expecting an asinine remark, and she didn't disappoint.

"Welcome, oh noble one, oh king of all the skies. I see you are conversing with some of your buzzing friends. I bet they are giving you an earful!"

Zeus knew he was being tested - even the king of the gods has to answer to the rules of eternity - and much as he felt like calling in a few thousand scorpions to teach her a lesson, he decided to be as nice as he could be given the current situation - especially remembering that his powers were suspect at best in this place.

"Yes, indeed, dear Pythia. They were saying how lucky they were to live in such a beautiful place with such a wonderful person."

"Flattery will get you nowhere, you big bag of wind. Let's get down to cases.

Follow me. And try not to destroy the rest of my place of business!"

CHAPTER NINE
THE PROPHECY??

Zeus followed her down a rocky and winding path, turning his ankle on a stone he swore she planted there deliberately. He struggled not to make a sound so she wouldn't realize anything was wrong. At least the hornets seemed to have disappeared, but Pythia's attitude was in its full unfurled mode.

"Let's go, your rotundness," she ordered. "I have other people coming, you know. Can't spend all day with you."

"One of these days, Pythia, I'm going to knock your block off," he thought to himself. He had never used that phrase before. He liked it, but he couldn't help but wonder where it had come from. Then he remembered that time and place were often jumbled and turned upside down in Dephi, and he correctly surmised that it was one of the thousands of pieces that came and went in this "den of the devil," another of his pet names for this place. Still, he noted it: he could use it again, perhaps with Hera. He didn't know it at the time but remembering something glib to say would be the least of his problems, as the things about to be revealed to him would make his head spin, literally.

The Oracle reached a secluded glade, pointed to a large rock, and ordered Zeus to sit down. He couldn't help himself as he sarcastically bowed his head and vowed that her wish was indeed his command. He knew she would get him back at some point, and she indicated as much by curling up the left part of her lip, but enough was enough.

"So, Poseidon tipped you off to come here, am I correct?" she queried.

"Why, yes, he did. Does that matter?" Zeus answered as politely as he could.

"Just want to get my facts straight. I like your brother." (As dumb as he is, she thought to herself. Ironically, Zeus was thinking the same thing). To refresh your memory, Poseidon is the god of the sea."

A scowl crossed Zeus's face. It was bad enough that he was here, but she was getting close to the line, and even though his powers diminished vastly in this hell hole, he could still punch her in the face. But he kept his composure as best he could.

"Yes, if memory serves."

The sarcasm was not lost on Pythia as, literally out of the blue, about a dozen angry bees buzzed within an inch of the god king's nose. She raised her eyebrows just a bit as a not-too-subtle sign that there were more where those came from.

"Shall I continue?" she asked with such a stern look on her face that, for a moment, Zeus thought she had turned into Hera. Oh, lord.

"Yes, go on," he answered as contritely as possible. Inside he was seething.

"Your brother has sometimes been, shall I say 'inaccurate,' with his tips, but I think in this case he is actually on to something, and it's big."

"Well, the last time you had me down here, it was because he thought he saw a ship loaded with all kinds of animals. And it turned out to be a bunch of sea otters living in the wreck of an old trading vessel."

"I admit he's had his share of missteps. He does live in the water, and that sometimes clouds his accuracy. But this time, he got the tip from two mermaids he knows and trusts, and I think he's got something very, very important!"

Pythia slowly raised her hands over her head, and the scent of incense permeated the air, filled with what appeared to be shimmering raindrops suspended over the mystic and the king. Zeus couldn't help but be impressed, although the "cauldron of fire" he often used as his calling card left Pythia's creation in the dust. Still, if nothing else, it got his attention.

"BEHOLD!" she announced, in a voice at least two octaves lower than any he'd ever heard - mortal, God, or anyone in between. He was so shocked he almost wet his pants.

There appeared in their midst a young woman, around twenty years old, he guessed, the most stunningly gorgeous maiden he had ever seen. If nothing else, Zeus was a connoisseur of the fairer sex and *having* sex with the fairer sex.

He was transfixed by her appearance and the aura of beauty she embodied.

"Please tell me who this is," he sincerely asked the Oracle.

"Well, some people claim she is your daughter--"

Zeus' eyes widened as he did a godly double take.

"But she is not. In fact, she has not yet been born, which will not happen for three months. Her name is Helen, Helen of Troy, and she will be known as the most beautiful woman in the world."

Pythia waved her hand, and Helen disappeared, replaced by another maiden, about the same age, swarthy and seductive, and equally as attractive. Zeus was overwhelmed by her beauty as well. He was about to say something when the Oracle put her finger to her lips to indicate that he should be quiet.

"This is Maria. She will be born in Sicily at just about the same time Helen will be born in Sparta." Pythia waved her hand, and Helen returned, standing within arm's length of Maria, "I ask you, oh king of the gods, which one is more beautiful??"

For probably the first time in his life, Zeus was speechless. All he could do was look back and forth from one to the other--and then back again--and again. He started to sweat profusely and then just kept shaking his head.

His first words were a question: "You said that the first one's name was Helen of Troy, but she will be born in Sparta?"

"I will get to that--just answer me: which one is more beautiful?"

He decided the only way to do it was to look at one at a time and see what features stood out. Helen was tall and slender, with a somewhat pale complexion for a Greek, yet her skin had a vibrancy that seemed to glow. Her hair was long and cascaded down past her shoulders, framing lips that were moist and inviting and dark, piercing eyes. Her shape was more than "ample," and it was hard to look away.

But when he did manage to look away, there was Maria, a dark, inviting image of a woman cloaked in mystery. She was voluptuous and provocative, and it was easy to get lost in her eyes. Of course, Zeus didn't know any of these descriptive phrases. He just knew she was hot. So was Helen. And he failed to see the problem, a sentiment he conveyed to his host. So, what if there were two more beautiful women in his domain? The more, the better.

With another wave of Pythia's hand, the two beauties disappeared, and Zeus snapped back into the present day.

"Tell me, oh mighty one, did you ever hear of any of these phrases: a Trojan Horse; the face that launched a thousand ships; the Odyssey?"

"Can't say that I have," Zeus answered matter of factly.

"Well, they haven't been uttered yet, but they will eventually become an everyday part of both history and the vocabulary of most of the world. You asked me about Helen? She's called Helen of Troy because she was taken to Troy, which led to a war with the Greeks. It was because she was the most beautiful woman in the world, not one of the most beautiful women in the world.

Zeus was still befuddled, which he often was. He hadn't become king of the gods by his thought processes. That's why there were others on Olympus to help him sort things out, particularly Hera and Athena. But they could hardly blame Zeus for his confusion about Helen and Maria.

Zeus liked a good battle as well as the next person, but so what if there was not to be another war? The Greeks were a quarrelsome group, and it might do them some good to take a war off with whomever it was to be. He didn't want to mess with things, especially beautiful women if he didn't have to. Running the universe was a tough job. One thing he had learned was not to create more problems when discretion would be a better option. Hmmm, he seemed to have heard a phrase about that - - well, maybe not. Anyway, messing with the natural order of things to protect a couple of words used in the future did not seem worth the fuss.

He expressed his quandary to the Oracle, who shook her head. He was expecting a vitriolic tongue lashing, but instead, she was calm and courteous and spoke in a businesslike, sincere tone. This caught Zeus by surprise, and he was a bit uneasy because he could deal with the callous way she normally treated him. But she was almost cordial. Something was wrong. He decided to play her game and see what happened. Sooner or later, he was sure she would revert to her old, nasty self. It turned out to be sooner.

"Now, my dear king of the gods, let me put this as simply as possible so even you can understand it."

For her part, even though this matter was of prime importance in the proper progression of life and history, she couldn't resist annoying him while she had the chance. But for once, Zeus used good judgment. Eager to get away from her as quickly as possible and not wanting to jeopardize any future visions she might send his way; he kept his head and was as nice as possible. So instead of firing back an epithet or otherwise remark to counter her sarcasm, he merely said: "sure, that sounds good to me." Pythia was speechless, which was extremely satisfying in and of itself. Besides, he would get even with her sometime over the next century or so—

"All right, then," she began. Still a bit shocked by Zeus's quiescence. "It's as easy as 1, 2 ,3; 1 - Without Helen as the most beautiful woman in the world, there would be no thousand ships, no Trojan War. 2 - Without the Trojan War, the Greeks would not have the same arrogance and pride, and imagination that became their trademark. 3 - Hence, no Homer, no Odyssey, no DEMOCRACY, no Hippocrates or Pythagoras, and the history of the world would not be as it should be."

Now, Zeus didn't quite get all her references. In fact, he had trouble following most of her explanation, but "not as it should be" caught his attention. He had enough trouble ruling over the mortals and the gods without having something he could prevent, making things worse.

"So," he asked very sincerely, "I need to do something about these two potential beauties. Is that the gist of it?"

"There it is, big guy," she answered sincerely. Surprisingly, there were no major earthquakes or cosmic disturbances, even though this was probably the first time in history that these two had exchanged consecutive remarks that could be considered cordial enough to be printed.

Zeus bid her a quick but proper goodbye and made a hasty exit, avoiding any potentially nasty bugs or vegetation. He felt the vision of the "chosen two," as he would call the two beautiful women, hovering in his soul, and he realized that both time and fate were working against him. Zeus could feel the pressure in every molecule of his body. He needed someone with great intellect to help him figure this out. He needed Athena!

CHAPTER TEN
IT'S JUST MARIA

As the period for lunch duty approached, Nick began to sweat more and more profusely, both figuratively and literally. If he told her that a dream was the reason for his behavior in the morning, she would think he had lost his grip on reality. Maybe if he said nothing, she would forget what he had been babbling about so incoherently. After all, this *was* the first day of school, the *real* first day, and even though she probably had all her stuff together, his comments may have slipped her mind by lunchtime. She did look a bit stressed, which is the norm for just about any teacher on the first day. On the other hand, Maria was pretty sharp, and it didn't seem that anything would slip by her. He would soon find out just how sharp she was in all aspects of her persona.

The bell rang, signaling the beginning of lunch. Nick didn't have to ask for whom the bells tolled: his name was written all over them, and the echo "Pappas...Pappas" seemed to resonate on and on as he walked down the hall toward the cafeteria. He was so preoccupied he didn't even notice stepping on the feet of at least two senior female faculty members and opening the door smack into the back of the principal. What a start to the year.

"Sorry, Mr. Morgan, I didn't see you there."

"Glad you're so anxious to get to your assignment," the principal sarcastically retorted as he dusted off his suit. Nick wished he had opened it harder. At least Maria wasn't there yet, so he had a few seconds to figure something out. Some people are good under the pressure of time; Nick wasn't.

"Hello, hello."

Holy shit, she was here already.

"Hi, Maria." When they passed out lines to say to beautiful women, Nick must have been either in the men's room or unconscious. "Hi, Maria." Please. A doorknob could have come up with a better line.

"Jesus Christ," he yelled at himself in frustration. He yelled it *at* himself but not *to* himself.

"What was that Nick?" Maria queried with a look on her face that one could only describe as unfair. He yelled an internal "holy shit" and punched himself in the leg as hard as he could. Here he was making a fool of himself, just like in his dream, and here she was, charming and enticing as ever.

"Sorry. My leg fell asleep, and I tried to get it going again. Sorry."

"Oh, no problem. I thought your anger was directed at me." This was one of the most effective of her ploys, and she would use it repeatedly during the year: turning things around so they would land on Nick. She did it so smoothly and effortlessly that there was no defense for it. None. All he could do was sit there like the dumb ass he portrayed so often and so well.

"Oh, no, no. Just some first-day frustrations and second guesses."

"Hey, I'm sorry I didn't have time to talk this morning, Nick. I had to run some things off, and I couldn't find a book I thought I had in my car. What was it you wanted to explain to me?"

"Well, uh, it was nothing. It got cleared up on its own," Nick answered half-heartedly.

What a break, he thought to himself. She hadn't paid much attention to his comment and was just being polite in asking him about it. Whew, he was off the hook. Or was he? Had she put it in the unimportant part of her day, or was she just pretending so she could make him squirm that much more? Most people would have just taken things at face value and been happy with the result. But not Nick. Second-guessing himself was an obsession, and when it involved something or someone important, it became a continuous mental demon that wouldn't quit. And, though he didn't realize it at the time, no one would become more important to him than Maria.

Much to Nick's amazement, after his initial clumsiness, lunchtime seemed to be progressing rather well. And he didn't even have the urge to say something stupid. Of course, most of the silly things he said started as rational, sometimes even clever, phrases when they were formulated in his brain. But something usually happened to them on their trip to his tongue. What had started as one innocent utterance often became another in the seemingly endless line of misstatements, he wished he could take back.

Maria was already busy as she attacked a pile of papers with a red pen and the eye of a Kentucky rifleman. Nick was in awe of how she read and evaluated every detail of a student's work and wrote comments faster than a sewing machine could complete a stitch. Nick had a completely different technique, captured in the saying he had concocted as a way to speed up the process: "Just a glance, then back to the dance." He would look at the kid's paper(usually) but just take in the general point, slap a grade onto it, and then grab the next one. Of course, he wasn't an English teacher, especially a Tasmanian Devil grader like Maria, so he could justify just getting the gist of things.

"Lot of stuff for the first day," he commented to make some conversation.

"Well, this is an Honors Class, so I figured they might as well get cracking," was the matter of fact answer that was pretty much a dead end as far as continuing the conversation.

Was she throwing up roadblocks to talking, did she have a lot of work to do, or was it him? Or some combination of the above? Man, he wished he had better skills when talking to beautiful women. "Better" skills? Whom was he kidding? He would have settled for "any" skills when talking to beautiful women.

His self-rapprochement was suddenly interrupted by a "Hey Nick" from the woman "next door."

"Huh?" he answered. Maria had caught him by surprise, and, in retrospect, it was probably one of the least reckless t things he would say over the next ten months. But of course, he wound up saying it twice--"Huh?"

"You looked like you were in deep thought.," Maria smiled. "Didn't mean to interrupt." She was laughing now. With him, at him, both? He wasn't in deep thought, he was in a deep mental mess, and, as usual, he had only himself to blame.

"No, just daydreaming a bit. What's up?"

"My pen just bit the dust. Can I borrow one?"

"Sure. Here, I've got a bunch in my briefcase."

In his haste to please, he grabbed the two handles of his case so forcefully that he wound up knocking over his computer and the pile of books sitting by Maria's right elbow. He profusely apologized as he gathered everything up.

"Don't worry about it," she managed to say through her exploding laughter. Well, at least now Nick knew at whom Maria directed her frivolity. It sort of broke the tension in his mind, and he started laughing at his clumsiness.

As he picked up her books, he uttered the first coherent thing he had said in several days.

"Hey, Maria, I'm Nick. Could we start this over?"

"I know who you are. Yeah, why not," she said with a smooth smile across her face. Nick smiled back, and it was then that he noticed her eyes. He had never seen anything like them before. They were, without a doubt, the most beautiful eyes Nick had ever seen, and they would be transfixed in his soul from that moment forward. But--damn it, he thought, why did there always have to be a "but" in things. Why couldn't he just take things as they were? Well, he had known the answer to that his whole life. He always, with few exceptions, would go back over just about everything he did: himself, his words, his actions, even his private thoughts. And with Maria, it would become a daily torment reviewing what had just transpired. BUT...in this case, the word was justified.

It was her eyes. As he sat there, he tried not to look at them and failed miserably. But there was something that for once would justify a "but." But what the hell was it? They sparkled as clearly as the north star, yet they were simultaneously sultry and mysterious. They were--they were to die for--that was it. That was what he had told Doug, that they were to die for. But wasn't that part of his dream? And if that were the case, had he seen them, perhaps during some other year, or had he merely imagined them in his nocturnal world?

Maria turned toward him just as the bell rang to end the period, and he saw them again.

"What's the matter, Nick? You look like you're in another world." If only she knew.

CHAPTER ELEVEN
TWO COLLEAGUES

Nick and Maria had been teaching together for a dozen years or so, and they would say hello from time to time, but their interaction was cursory at best, and they didn't know that much about each other. That would soon change as, over the next few days, they conversed about everything from who they were to what TV shows they liked.

First of all, there was no getting away from the fact that she was stunning to look at. On "dress down" days, Maria looked good - no, better than good. But when she "dressed" for school, which was every other day, she was devastating. There was one outfit in particular that stood out in his mind and would give him cold sweats when he thought about it. It was a tan (beige?) skirt with a matching top and brown boots to go with it. Holy smokes - how was he supposed to concentrate on anything, much less behave matter-of-factly in dealing with the everyday activities required of a teacher? Nick was a bit emotional and given to flights of imagination. Nick had this "goddess" sitting next to him every day would have been a tough assignment for even an n average person. So, this was genuinely unimaginable for a sometimes irrational and often fanciful Greek. And this was just the "cover" of the book. Ironically, as gorgeous as she was to look at, it turned out that her intellect superseded her appearance and her soul, both of which he would encounter daily and would quickly change his entire life.

Nick knew right off the bat that he was out of his league and that his penchant for letting his heart direct his actions would lead to trouble more often than not. It had done so already, and this was only the start of his duty with her. So, he decided that in one area, at least, he would stay on the straight and narrow - and that was propriety. He promised himself that no matter what else happened over the course of the next few days and months, he would *never* allow himself to say or even *think of* anything unseemly or inappropriate. He was as good as his word, and. It wasn't easy. He was tested almost immediately. Maria had a habit of going around the cafeteria and checking to ensure things were kept relatively neat. Every once in a while, she would stop and gently urge someone to tidy up or pick something up off the floor. Sometimes she would pitch in and help clean up a table or even bend over to pick a wrapper up off the floor herself. As soon as he spotted her about to do this, Nick looked away. It was his only defense, but he still needed a cold shower.

Maria had taught for several years in California, and Nick assumed that was where she was from. For once, instead of beating around the bush or trying to surmise her origins from conversations, refreshingly, he thought to himself, he would just ask her, and he did.

"So, where did you teach in California?"

"LA," was her succinct reply. Maria did not waste words, pretty much the opposite of Nick, although he managed to stick to the topic in this conversation at least.

"Are you from out there?"

"Nope, I'm a Jersey Girl."

"Oh, yeah, I think you already told me, sorry."

"I told you that? I don't think so. You must be thinking of two other Jersey girls," she said with a big smile followed by an infectious laugh.

Nick offered an "Oh yeah" and a halfhearted grin in response. She was right. He couldn't have known she was from Jersey until just now. But he couldn't shake the feeling that they already had had this conversation.

For once in his life, he was right. They had had the same exchange of ideas in his dream. Holy shit. This time, he said it to himself.

And was she ever a Jersey girl. The more he got to "know" her, the more he could see the "Jersey" in her. (n.b. - "know" is in quotes because as this is being written, just about a year after the two of them met on lunch duty, Nick still can't figure her out, which is part of her charm and mystique...), or was it the Sicilian in her? Well, even an idiot like Nick, overwhelmed with a thousand emotions, could see that it was both. She was feisty, quick-witted, unafraid, and unflappable, and at the same time, she could be passionate and kindhearted - although she did her best to hide her soft side. What was that his friend from across the hall had said: "good to look at but watch out"? Wait, was that part of the dream? Well, dream or not, he was right. As Nick would find out, it was not a good idea to get on Maria's bad side 'cause she could charm you with her engaging smile and stick a knife in your back simultaneously. Of course, Nick's heritage was from a Mediterranean island as well, albeit a Greek one, and he could relate to these dark side traits quite easily, having witnessed similar ones in many people he met as he was growing up. But none of them could even come close to the comely Sicilian sitting to his left.

But being familiar with these characteristics and being able to deal with Maria were two different things entirely. She was like no one Nick had ever met, nor would ever meet. Nick had some redeeming qualities but dealing with people, even just garden variety, everyday individuals, was not one. How the hell would he be even slightly lucid and coherent with someone like Maria? And that last statement was unnecessarily wordy. There was no one *like* Maria - there was just Maria! Nick's musings were interrupted by the sound of someone calling his name.

"Nick, Nick. Mr. Pappas!"

Was this another goddamn dream? No, it was the goddamn principal. Nick tried to shake the cobwebs out of his head and make himself appear as if he, at least partially, gave a shit.

"Hey, Mr. Morgan. Just thinking about my next class. What's up?"

Maria could barely contain herself and coughed into tissue to cover her laughter. "You OK, Maria," Nick asked, genuinely concerned. The glance he got in return allayed his fears, and he had to bite his tongue to stop from bursting out into a cascade of chuckles himself.

"Nothing major. Just wanted to be sure that you got the email regarding going to the media center. It will not be open till next week, so please don't give out any passes."

"We got it," Nick responded blandly, keeping the rest of his thought, "you frickin' jerk," to himself.

"Good. I just wanted to be sure. Have a good day," the school leader responded as he briskly did an about-face and walked away. Principal Morgan was new to the school. He had been principal in the district's middle school, but high school is another animal, both in the student population and the staff. He presented a professional appearance, bald head notwithstanding, but suddenly he began to wear orange ties, which did not enhance his image as a high school principal. He was a stickler for the tiniest detail, and it remains unclear if he would have the teachers' backs since he also had a reputation for following directives from higher up to the letter! He's also apparently thin-skinned and would take offense at the slightest provocation.

Nick's disdain for Morgan was evident. It wasn't so much that he didn't like him but didn't trust him. Morgan would tell you one thing in the morning and then something different in the afternoon, depending on whom he had talked to in the interim. Nick was doubly angry because the damn principal interrupted his thoughts about his lunch duty partner.

Nick quickly restored his as Maria nudged him with her elbow-- ah, the touch of a goddess, he thought to himself, Jersey girl or not. He smiled at the metaphor. She was much better than a goddess, but that was something he wouldn't find out till a bit later in this odyssey.

"Is he a piece of work, or what?" Maria offered as a return to their conversation.

"I've got a good mind to give everyone here a pass to the Media Center," Nick responded. "So, where in Jersey are you from, Maria?"

"I grew up in Hillsfield, not too far from here. Ever been there?"

"Ever been there? I used to take piano lessons there. Do you know where Werner Street is?"

"Werner Street? That's where our house is. My mother still lives there," Maria answered incredulously, as slight disbelief spread across her face. "How long did you take lessons?"

"All through high school. Wow, maybe I saw you a time or two. Quite a coincidence."

Nick tried to contain his real emotions, which were now up and running in different directions. He felt that many things passed off as coincidences were part of some master plan, a grand scheme of things, if you will, for the universe and its inhabitants. Of course, many people felt that things like this were mere chance, but there were eighty teachers in the school, and he wound up with a person in his life who would change it in ways he could not even imagine. And now there was this thing with his piano lessons. He still had the same damn piano.

"To think you could have been playing in your yard when I was playing on the piano just a few doors away." He laughed at his own joke, and Maria grimaced.

"You can do better than that--I would hope, Nick."

"Well, five will get you ten on that one. But, to be honest, this is intriguing. To say the least. I feel a little like George Bailey."

"George Bailey?" Maria queried.

"Yeah, you know, from *It's a Wonderful Life.*"

"Know it? That's my favorite movie!"

"Yeah, mine too!" said Nick, so loudly that kids at the first table turned their heads. "Favorite movie, favorite actor—"

"OMG…Jimmy Stewart." Maria gasped. "Me, too."

Nick tried to change venues and the medium, if for no other reason than to keep from having some kind of meltdown or stroke. "What about TV? I mean, what shows do you like?"

"I love *The Honeymooners*—"

"That's my favorite show," Nick practically screamed. "This is getting like *The Twilight Zone*—"

"I've seen every episode," Maria responded.

"Me, too," Nick answered incredulously. "What's your favorite?"

"How about the one we seem to be in right now, Nick?!?"

He could only shake his head in agreement and disbelief as the bell rang.

YIKES!!!

CHAPTER TWELVE
SAY WHAT?

Nick made his way slowly back to his room, his head spinning with what had just transpired, not to mention "the dream" about Maria and his first day of school. It was hard for him to figure out whether what he dreamt mirrored reality or if it were the other way around. In contrast to his excessive nocturnal miles per hour, he seemed to be moving slower than a fence post, and several seniors made lighthearted comments about his age catching up with him. This usually would have resulted in a few good-natured expletives, but he was too caught up in what had just happened to give a rat's ass. Nick edged into his room, dropped his briefcase on his desk, grabbed his bat, and walked into the hall just as the late ball sounded. "Shit," he said semi quietly under his breath. Nick hoped to have a minute to get his head together, but today the gods of time were against him. Then he had an inspiration. He leaned into his room, slammed the bat on a vacant desk, and announced that a quiz would commence in three minutes.

"Mr. Pappas, how can we have a quiz on the first day," asked a rather hefty kid from the back row.

"You'll see very shortly, my man," Nick retorted in the most authoritative voice he could muster.

Nick was often at a loss for words when dealing with one, especially when the other was female, particularly when the other was Maria. But in front of a class, he could change things on the fly and bullshit with the best of them, so even though he had no inkling of what he was going to throw at his students, he knew that an idea would come to him, and it did.

"OK, take out a piece of paper and something to write with. Number from one through fifteen and leave a space between each line."

A hand went up in the far corner.

"Yeah, Max, what?"

"Mr. Pappas, does it matter whether we use pen or pencil?"

"Your choice. OK, listen, so I don't have to repeat this. For numbers 1-5, list five states you would like to visit and tell why. Then, for 6-10, write down five famous people in history and why they were famous. Lastly, for 11-15, make up your own questions on anything to do with history. I'll give you about 19 minutes. THINK. It's an easy good grade. Got it?"

There were no other questions, which was fairly astonishing, but even more astonishing was that this shoot from the hip assignment wasn't half bad. Nick suppressed a smile and popped a peppermint lifesaver into his mouth. Peppermint is supposed to help you think, and Nick surely needed some big-time assistance right about now. Well, he always needed some, as Jim would say. Between the opening of school, his newly found acquaintance, and his apparent journey into another universe, he was more frazzled than usual. Although Nick knew he had to cut down, he poured another cup of coffee, grabbed his Mickey Mantle Louisville Slugger 34" bat, and sat on the stool next to his desk. He opened up a bag of cookies and invited the class to help themselves. He often did this on a Friday, and since he had thought today *was* Friday, he figured why not.

Now, what the hell was going on? He retraced the last couple of days - or was it just the previous day - to see if he could make any sense of it all, or, for that matter, of any of it. One thing you had to say about Nick Pappas was that he was consistent. When he was on a roll, there was no one better. And when he was confused and bewildered, there was no one dumber. The class was cooperating - busily and silently working.

They even ate the cookies quietly. A good atmosphere for thinking. The problem was that Nick didn't even know where to start. Was it all real? Did all these things happen? Did some of them happen? Did none of them happen? For all he knew, he was dreaming (read *hallucinating*) right now. He got up to get more coffee, and he noticed a book on his desk. It was *The Odyssey*. Where did that come from? It looked like a pretty nice edition, but it wasn't his. He picked it up and looked inside, and the mystery was solved. On the inside of the cover, written in red, was the owner's name: *Maria Orlando*. "Lord. She must have had it at lunch, and I picked it up with all my stuff," he thought aloud. "She's gonna think I took it deliberately."

"Did you say something, Mr. Pappas?" Diane wondered.

She was sitting in the corner seat of the last row. Nick figured that if she heard him, everyone had heard him. He was correct.

"Who's gonna think you took what?" said a voice from the other corner.

"Yeah, what are you up to, Pappas," joshed a student Nick had known since he was in second grade.

"All right, all right. I took another teacher's book at the end of lunch duty. By mistake. No big deal."

"What was the book?" queried another bright-eyed young man.

"What difference does it make?"

"Just trying to get all the facts, Mr. Pappas. Isn't that what a historian does?"

Said a smiling blond in the front row.

"OK, for what it's worth, it's *The Odyssey*," Nick answered with a feigned frown.

"That's pretty heavy stuff, Pappas. Trojan Horse and Helen of Troy. Didn't know you were into the classics," his old acquaintance chuckled. "Who is the teacher you stole it from?"

"I didn't steal it. I took it by mistake, you knuckleheads." By this time, everyone was laughing, including Nick.

"The teacher?" a nameless face asked again.

"OK, OK--it was Ms. Orlando," Nick answered innocently. The tone of the class changed just a bit.

"You're in deep shit, man," laughed Jeremy from the front row.

Was he ever!

CHAPTER THIRTEEN
IT'S TOUGH BEING KING

Zeus slowly made his way back to Mt. Olympus and climbed the thousands of steps to the summit. Of course, he could have been there with the speed of a thunderbolt, but if he had dreaded seeing the oracle, which was always mind-numbing, what he hated, even more was making important decisions. This one looked like a gut-wrenching one, if there ever was one. He reasoned that if he took his time returning to his often-problem plagued throne, some inspiration might come his way. To paraphrase Thomas Edison, it was not inspiration but perspiration that found a home with him, as the day was as muggy as the inside of a cave in July. Where the hell was the sun to burn off some of the humidity?

When he reached the top, his better half could see by the look on his face and the hundred or so bite marks on his neck and cheeks that things had not gone well. What she was about to tell him would most assuredly make a bad day worse, so she thought she would start gently with a smile and a compliment.

"You know, dear, all that walking you've been doing is certainly paying off. You're starting to trim down nicely: just like when we first met."

Although she was a lot smarter than her husband when it came to reading people and getting them to do what she wanted, she whiffed every once in a while, and this was one of those times. The truth was that Zeus had dropped some poundage, and he did look more like the young rogue he was when they met, but he was not buying the flattery at face value. Something was up, and he dreaded what would happen when the other shoe dropped. (Of course, the gods didn't wear shoes per se, and neither did anyone else, but the king was comfortable with the analogy, so why shouldn't we be?) But he didn't want to force a fight since, lord knows, they seemed to find him, so he decided to play along as best he could.

"Well, thank you, dear," he replied tersely. "It was a long morning with that woman, so I thought the exercise might clear my mind and erase the aftertaste of dealing with her. You're not going to believe this, but I think 'Seidon was onto something. I have some big decisions to make if what she showed me was on the up and up, although, quite frankly, I'm not sure why I need to make any decision. Wanna hear about it? You know that I value your opinion."

Zeus was telling somewhat of a half-truth, for although he did talk things over with his wife quite often, what he usually did was listen to her opinion and then do the opposite. But this time, he was at a loss, and he really did want to hear what Hera had to say. However, there was still another bridge to cross.

"Yes, dear, of course, I want to hear about it. But something came up while you were gone that I think you need to turn your attention to."

He forced a smile and a terse thank you and then braced himself for what most assuredly would be something he didn't want to hear. Despite his trepidation, Zeus had to chuckle to himself. Everyone wants to be the top dog, but as someone would say in a few thousand years, "it's lonesome at the top." It was not only lonesome, but it was often, pardon the pun, a royal pain in the ass or the neck, as was the case today.

"OK, what is it?"

Hera knew that the following would probably set her husband off, but she figured she might as well be done with it.

"The wine rep was here to see you."

Most people, even historians, don't realize that there were special interest groups even in those days and that each group had lobbyists petitioning the gods for this or that. There were the olive growers, the herders, the ship owners, the winemakers – just to name a few. Some of the reps were sociable and cordial, and Zeus and the other gods in charge liked them and looked forward to their visits. And then there was Vasilie Triandos, the wine rep, who, according to Zeus, was the most despicable human who had ever lived – or would ever live. If it weren't for the "no-kill" mandate, he might be visiting Hades rather than Mt. Olympus. Normally the king would have been glad to have missed Triandos' visit. Still, he knew he would be back, and if at all possible, he wanted to take care of any minor issues before turning his attention to the oracle's vision, which was still whirring around in his head. But he needn't have worried; his nemesis was still around. He was "visiting" Aphrodite, who for some reason seemed to like him, which was another thing Zeus could never figure out. How in the world could the goddess of beauty, his flesh, and blood no less, be attracted to this loud-mouthed, balding, middle-aged grape grower. He had heard the phrase "all the good ones go for jerks." He couldn't place it, but it was a fair statement. It would be uttered countless times by guys in the 20th Century, and of course, Zeus couldn't place it because it was 3,000 years in the future (a story for another day).

Lost in his thoughts, Zeus did not hear the laughter getting closer, and all at once, he looked up to see "beauty and the beast," as he had named them, unknowingly predating but accurately naming what would become an oft-told legend and story. Aphrodite smiled and did a half curtsy that she knew her father loved. Triandos bowed from the waist, which would typically be a sign of respect, but it was just his way of letting Zeus know that he wanted something, which he usually did.

"Good morning, ruler of all the heavens and earth. I am glad I did not have to leave before talking with you. How are you today, my benefactor and partner?"

Zeus had a good mind to knock him over the mountain with one swing, but he caught Hera's death stare and got control of himself. However, he couldn't resist a backhanded comment.

"I was doing all right until about thirty seconds ago. What can I do for you, show you the way down the mountain, perhaps? Find you a river filled with poisonous snakes? Arrange a guided tour of Hades?"

Triandos hadn't become the spokesman for the winemakers, the most powerful lobby in ancient Greece, by accident. He could read people and gods as well as anyone, and he knew that whatever brains the headman had were in some kind of turmoil, so he decided to take the high road.

"How was the wine I brought up a few days ago? That Sicilian red is out of this world, isn't it? Get it--out of this world?"

Usually, this approach would have worked to calm the big guy down. However, the mention of wine reminded Zeus about his hangover, which was still "hanging over" him. The Sicilian reference brought back his just completed visit to Delphi, which worsened his headache. He began to rotate his right arm, somewhat as a pitcher does before warming up. If you were anywhere in his vicinity, it usually meant that you would take the part of the ball and be hurtled somewhere at 95 mph plus. And Zeus did have a great throwing arm. (Of course, there was no baseball than to use it in.) Luckily, Hera cut in.

"Perhaps you could tell us exactly what brought you here today, and we can take it under consideration."

This seemed to break the growing tension. Zeus popped a few figs in his mouth, and his unwelcome guest assumed a very businesslike demeanor.

"A good idea, Mrs. H. You always seem to get us all going in the right direction." Hera nodded a sincere thank you, and her husband just rolled his eyes. Aphrodite was just sitting quietly and attentively.

"Your majesty, do you remember the 20/20 deal we made a few weeks ago? It was basically sun for wine."

His client looked puzzled, which he often did, but this was too important to leave to his often fragile mental facilities.

"Let me go over it quickly and simply, your highnesses. If I may?"

"Please do," Hera interjected.

"I know your two favorite wines are Sicilian Chianti and Robolo from Kefalonia. They are, without a doubt, two of the best my growers can produce. However, we are approaching a critical time of year, and both crops need twenty – that's a big two zero – straight days of sun for the grapes to mature properly. The deal was twenty consecutive days of sun for twenty free, that's no charge, barrels of each wine."

All this talk of alcoholic beverages was turning the king's stomach. Luckily, Hera knew about these two varieties and liked them quite a bit. She had been well taught by Dionysius, the god of wine, or Dion, as she called him. Zeus liked them as well, but in reality, wine was wine to the big guy, especially if someone else was paying the tab. She wanted to get all this taken care of before moving on to prophecies and other godly duties. She knew you couldn't run a good party, or a good anything, without good wine!

"All right, Vasilie, what can we do for you?"

"Well, the twenty days of sun were supposed to start today, and, as you can see, it's cloudy as hell, if you'll pardon my French."

Everyone looked around at the obvious: an overcast sky with not a speck of sun in sight. Of course, there were sunless days built into the yearly calendar, but apparently, this was not supposed to be one of them. A deal was a deal.

"Could the twenty days begin tomorrow?" Hera asked politely.

"They could, I guess. But after that, you run into the storms of the fall, and they would ruin the harvest."

All this time, Zeus had been quiet. The king's way of making his point was more often than not a right cross to the chin, so he thought it would be smarter to let his better half do the talking. His wife was a lot sharper, and she could be diplomatic and still get her point across without causing any bodily harm. He couldn't stomach Triandos even on a good day, and he nodded thanks to Hera as she continued.

"I can see why you're concerned. I promise you that someone will take care of it within the hour. Have a safe journey home. Can you find your way down?"

The last question was uttered more sternly, and Triandos knew he'd better get moving. The queen had given her word, which was good enough for him. And he learned from more than one visitor to Olympus that once she asked if you could find your way down, if you value your health, you'd better find your way down! This was the first time he had heard it personally, and he was not about to cross the real ruler of the heavens.

Triandos bid farewell with all the courtesy he could muster, bowed graciously, and set off on his return trek. Mission accomplished.

Now for the other business of the day.

CHAPTER FOURTEEN
WHERE IS THE DAMN SUN??

"Where is that lazy son of mine?"

Zeus was starting to get back to his old self, and he was fuming. He was just beginning to unwind just a bit after dealing with the oracle, his headache, and the everyday chores of being the top guy, and the last thing he needed was the visit from the wine worm, as Zeus referred to him. If Apollo had done his job, it would have been one less annoyance, and the god who towed the sun was in deep trouble.

"Apollo, where are you?" His voice thundered up and down Mount Olympus, but Apollo was nowhere to be found. He hadn't been at the party, so he couldn't have been hungover unless he had been drinking on his own, which was strictly forbidden. So, where were his wayward son and the wayward sun?

"Maria!" Hera suddenly called out!

"Say what?" Zeus belted out as his head snapped a quick one hundred eighty degrees.

"Maria. He just met a nymph named Maria. He's been talking a lot about her. I'll bet he's with her!"

"And he doesn't feel the need to confide in his father?"

"Well, dear, he didn't appreciate your flirting with the last two girls he brought by. And I think he really likes this one. He calls her '3S' for short."

Zeus' headache was starting to return full force. This often happened even without wine when he was trying to think about something new or when he was trying to think at all.

"HUH?"

"Swarthy, seductive, Sicilian."

"You mean she's not even Greek? Where the hell did he find her?"

"My guess is Sicily. And that's probably where he is."

Sicily. Why did that word sound familiar? And then it hit him: the oracle--and the island--SICILY. And wait, what was the name of that potential rival for Helen? MARIA!

The big guy was beaming that he figured it out on his own and all in his head. Of course, as he often did, he assumed that anyone else in the vicinity had been privy to his private thought processes. This was annoying to everyone in his inner circle, so to speak, but particularly to his wife, who had to put up with it constantly.

"I got it!" he exclaimed proudly. "What do you think?"

Hera gave him "the look," and he realized she had no idea what he was talking about, so he filled her in. His wife listened attentively and nodded slightly a time or two.

"OK, dear, let me see if I got this straight," she started. "The name Maria and the fact that she's from Sicily are important--and it's important because?"

"Because of what my brother found out and what that damn woman told me this morning. Don't you remember?" And then Zeus smacked himself on the forehead as it suddenly dawned on him that he hadn't told his wife anything about the prophecy, a realization corroborated by the fire shooting out of her eyes. He could feel it burning into his flesh.

"Whoops," was the second thing he said. The first was a thousand apologies – literally. He told Hera about the prophecy – well, as much as he remembered. His wife was silent, and then a thoughtful and somewhat worried look seemed to pervade her entire countenance.

"My love, are you sure about all this?"

Hera called her husband "my love" only at the far ends of the seriousness spectrum. She was either kidding or deeply concerned over something of earthshaking importance. Zeus could tell she wasn't kidding.

"As sure as I can be. I mean, I'm never at my best when I'm in Delphi, but I can tell you this for sure the Sicilian's name is Maria. I'd put my hand on a Bible if we had such a thing."

Hera still looked puzzled, and justifiably so.

"You think I'm nuts, don't you?"

"No, dear, this all sounds plausible, but how could Apollo's Maria be the same one in the prophecy if she is still unborn?"

"Well, wait. Obviously, she's not the same one. All those damn Italians are named Maria. I think it's the only female name they know." Hera was nodding her head.

"You know, you might be right, dear. You might be right."

The two of them broke into a pensive silence as they considered the possibility that the big guy was spot on with his analysis!

Suddenly the stillness was shattered by a young, vibrant, excited voice!

"Hey Pop! Wait till I tell you about this new girl I met!!"

It was Apollo!

CHAPTER FIFTEEN
"IT'S JUST A MATTER OF TIME"

Zeus was glad to see his son for a disparate variety of reasons, not the least of which was to give him a good what for, which seemed like the logical place to start.

"Where have you been? Where is the sun? The damn wine guy was here--you know how I hate him. Well?"

Normally getting chewed out by the head guy put the fear of the gods into anyone who was the target of the tirade, but Apollo just stood there calm as could be, with a big smile on his face.

"I spent some time with the most remarkable woman in the world. That's where I was, with Maria. If you ever saw her, you'd understand. What a woman!"

While Apollo knew that his father had a soft spot in his heart for just about any good-looking female, he was sincere in his adoration and was not trying to play on his dad's weakness for women. Nevertheless, leading off with his latest squeeze worked to his advantage, for his father was immediately intrigued, shown by the huge grin that started to form across his face. He didn't forget about the tongue lashing he was about to give, but his demeanor noticeably changed. Hera half smiled and just shook her head, for she knew her husband and what his first comments would be.

"Well, as I always say, if you're gonna shirk your duties, a woman is the best excuse – especially a good-looking woman. You just met her, and you seem taken with her. Well, that doesn't forgive your no-show with the sun the last couple of days, but the same thing has happened to me a time or two over the years. Just be sure that you can still perform your duties as well as pursue this 'lady de jure.'"

Zeus said this with a wistful look on his face. He as he began to reminisce about his pursuit of the fairer sex over the past decades. Hera somehow managed to keep a straight face when her husband said, "a time or two." Still, in the interests of civilization, she did not want to start a rhubarb when there was no need to, and she tried to get Zeus back to the prophecy, which had slipped to his back burner. To do that, she had to be sure their son got the sun going again on the morrow so the wine guy would stay in the vineyards where he belonged. She knew it would be tough enough for her husband to deal with this cataclysmic event the oracle had predicted without having his attention diverted by the sun's disappearance. Of course, Apollo was still young, and his youth often led to irresponsibility. She wasn't sure what led to her husband's irresponsibility, but she knew it was up to her to save the universe.

"But father, she's not--" Apollo began, but Hera cut him off.

"Before we get to this maiden of yours, Pol, we have to get something straightened out."

"Huh?" Apollo asked.

"Huh?" Zeus echoed.

She knew it. The Oracle and the prophecy had utterly left his mind. The mention of femininity and beauty in the same sentence left her husband at the mercy of his libido.

"Here's the deal, so pay attention, both of you." Hera was the boss, and Zeus knew it. She let him be the big shot and flaunt hit title and power, but she put her foot down on critical issues, and whenever she said "pay attention," it was time to shut up and listen. Both the king and his son snapped their heads in her direction and stopped talking.

"All right, gentlemen, here's the deal. Pol, your father made a pact with the 'wine worm,' as he calls him. Twenty straight days of sun for twenty free and delivered barrels of his two best wines."

"From Kefalonia and Sicily," Apollo added matter of factly.

"Precisely," Hera continued. "Now, normally, that wouldn't be a huge deal, but it looks like something big is coming up, and your father needs to focus his attention on how to handle it without worrying about that pesky Greek coming up here every other day. The twenty days of the sun were supposed to start today, but, of course, 'someone' was not on the job, was he?"

Apollo hung his head.

"Sorry about that," he said sincerely.

"Apology accepted," Hera said on behalf of both her and Zeus. "But you must give us your word that you will be pulling that ball of fire across the sky for the next twenty days. We are excited for you about your new squeeze, but she has to come second, at least for now. Agreed?"

Apollo nodded!

"And you, oh king of the hill, you need to get back to taking care of business, got it?"

Zeus knew that she was right, and although he was dying to hear about this new flame of Apollo's, he did have a lot of responsibility to take care of now.

All he could say was, "yes, dear, I know you're right," a phrase uttered millions of times by husbands since the beginning of time.

Apollo promised that both he and the sun would be on the road first thing in the morning, and the royal couple felt that they had made their point with the young buck, and there was no use scolding him any further. They were anxious to hear about his "new friend," but they had to get some handle on this potential crisis Poseidon had uncovered. Since the day was pretty well-shot weather-wise, they asked the chariot driver to hang around. The more heads they could get together for this, the better.

But the smartest goddess on the mountain was still nowhere to be found. Where the blazes was Athena? They didn't realize that that's precisely where she was. Athena's location was a moot point, so they decided to go on without the important fourth wheel of their think tank.

Hera decided that a libation was in order before they sat down to some serious discussion. She got a coffee for herself despite a plea for some "light" wine and spring water for the big guy. Apollo, who was still a young kid in her eyes, received a big mug of goat's milk, despite his request for something a bit more adult.

"It's good for your bones, young man. What if someday you fall out of that ramshackle chariot of yours? You know, I was never crazy about your job, to begin with!"

Apollo was about to protest, but a quick glare from Zeus stopped him in his tracks. Besides, he was curious to see what his father had to say about what Poseidon had supposedly uncovered; and he wanted to brag about his "new friend," as they called her. Friend? He chuckled to himself. Despite his "youth," he had been around the block –around the world – a time or two, and she was the most stunning female he had ever encountered. She kept him going through those long treks across the sky, and it was hard to suppress a smile as he sipped his milk.

As was usually the case, Hera got things started. "OK, let's get down to business. If you can stop thinking about that woman for a few minutes and wipe that shit-eating grin from your face, perhaps your father can do the same." How Hera knew Zeus was thinking about Apollo's girlfriend was beyond him, but she knew, oh, she knew, so he deliberately bit his tongue so that a look of concern replaced the smile.

"I'm good to go, my love," he offered, tongue in cheek.

"It's all yours," his wife replied. She waved her hand grandly as an introduction.

Zeus related every moment of his visit to Delphi, and for someone whose forte never had been details, he managed to cover all that she told him and everything else that had transpired. He related his battle with the hornets and the supposed insolence of the oracle as well, things that were admittedly not relevant, but he was on such a roll that Hera was afraid that if she stopped him, he would lose his train of thought and leave something out. After what seemed like a small eternity, Zeus took one final deep breath and let out a loud "whew," indicating he was done. Hera and Apollo gave him a sincere round of applause and rewarded Zeus with some espresso and baklava.

"Well," he continued. "What do you think?"

"I wish I could have been there to see your battle with the hornets," Apollo threw in with the smile back on his face.

Zeus took the kidding in stride and promised he would take care of them the next time their paths crossed.

Hera brought things back to the issue at hand as was her wont.

"That's quite a story, dear. Do you think that your brother – for once – is on to something?"

"My gut tells me he is. But I'm still confused. Except for bragging rights, does it matter whether or not this Helen of Troy is the most beautiful woman in the world? I mean, who cares? And apparently, she's not from Troy. She's from Sparta. Plus, she hasn't even been born yet. Very confusing."

Apollo was scratching his head, which was not unusual given his daily journey through the clouds, but now he was trying to put things together. Hera sat with one hand on her chin, much like the Thinker statue from thousands of years in the future. The king and his son knew enough not to bother her when she got into this pose since it usually meant that there was some answer forthcoming; and that the retribution for disturbing her would be a pain in the ass. She had several hundred pains as she had her own private swarm of wasps at the ready. Zeus had had enough battles with insects for one day, and the truth of the matter was that he was not in the mood to cross his wife at this particular time, especially when he so desperately needed her help.

Hera broke the silence with a question, soon followed by several more. (The word on the street is that Socrates got his so-called "Socratic Method" by studying Hera's technique, but that's neither here nor there.)

"Here's my question," Hera began. "First of all, do we know that this is all on the level, or are your brother and Pythia getting even for your starting the rumor last summer that the ocean was drying up and Poseidon was being reassigned as the god of the deserts?"

Zeus was about to answer when she waved her hand to indicate that she didn't need his input. His wife's countenance was still sternly serious, and he had to suppress his grin and laughter at the mention of that prank. He really had his brother going. Of course, they had polished off almost a barrel of wine just between the two of them, and 'Seidon was so gullible a child could have sold him a container of saltwater to help prevent the demise of the ocean. Come to think of it, his brother began stocking up on them--bottles of water, not children. The king's reverie was interrupted by a sharp smack on the head.

"Pay attention! Sometimes I wonder which of the two brothers is the dumb one. This is important stuff." Zeus nodded sheepishly. His wife continued while Zeus and Apollo nodded inwardly and shot a knowing glance at each other. "Answering my own question, I doubt if Poseidon would be smart enough to come up with something so clever, and this is not Pythia's style. So, we have to assume that what she told you was true to the best of her knowledge."

"Next—" Hera went on and on with about a dozen very precise and critical questions, none of which appeared to have any answers, at least from the information available to them at the moment. "The bottom line is whether this prophecy is legitimate and why, as you so eloquently put it, does it matter so much. What we need is more time to consider this."

"What we need is Athena!" Zeus interjected.

They all agreed to table the discussion until the goddess of wisdom showed up, whenever that might be. Apollo was still dying to tell them about his latest love, and Hera figured that they might as well let him since often a problem can be better solved if you get away from it for a bit. Hera turned to Apollo.

"So, dear, who is this new babe you're all wrapped up in?"

A coast-to-coast smile formed on the young god's face, and it was plain to see that he was bursting with exuberance, enthusiasm, and even some erotic ideas, although he would deny the latter when asked.

"Well, she's about this tall," holding his hand up palm down at about five feet three or so to indicate her height, "with dark hair, a mysterious smile, and the most beautiful eyes I've ever seen."

Zeus was interested immediately, and Hera had to remind him that this was Apollo's maiden, not another nymph to invite to his wine marathons.

"I was just trying to show the boy some support, my love," he said with such good humor that Hera gave him a big smooch on his cheek. If nothing else, the change in subject had lightened the mood quite a bit; the tension that had enveloped everyone's conversation replaced with a light-hearted playfulness befitting a family of gods, or any family, for that matter.

"So, tell us some more. What is she like? How did you meet? What is her name?" his father asked with a sincerity and clarity that caused Apollo and Hera to do a double-take. Of course, her name had already been posted, as it were, but neither his wife nor son wanted to take away from the father's moment of at least semi clarity. Zeus just shrugged them off and told his son to continue. After dealing with Pythia, the hornets, and Triandos, relaxing was just what he needed. Say what you want to about Zeus – and many gods and mortals did – when he was in a good mood, there was no one you'd want to be around more. Of course, these episodes of joviality were often of limited duration, as there would usually be something that would short circuit the good humor. And that something was about to emerge.

"Well, it's kind of funny how we met - almost as if fate had taken a hand." Zeus lifted his head slightly when he heard the word "fate," as it conjured up his tussle with Pythia that very morning, but he was anxious to hear about this new chick, so he brushed it off.

"Go ahead, son, get to the good stuff."

"Well, I was rolling along through the heavens just about to head into a bank of clouds, so I eased up on the reins and gave my steeds a rest. I glanced down and saw a flickering light. It looked like some sort of signal, and since I was close to Delphi, I wanted to take a closer look and see what was up with Pythia - and I was so happy that I did."

The king was about to interrupt when a slight wave of Hera's hand stopped him cold. She smiled and quickly interjected, "Go ahead, Pol, we're all ears."

"—so, I get down there, and she can't move because her foot is stuck in a crack in a cave wall. Luckily, she just happened to have a mirror with her and was able to flash for help."

The image of his adversary trapped in her own lair, as it were, was too much for the king, and he burst out laughing as he pictured her struggling to get free. And it was no secret why she just "happened to have" a mirror with her. She was so full of herself that she constantly had to see her reflection no matter what else was going on. She would hide it in her robes if she had a visitor, right off her hip. When she was alone, it was right up in her face. This was too much! A narcissistic, egotistical, overbearing wench wedged into rocks. Tears were coming down his cheeks, and the more he tried to stop, the louder and more raucous his laughter became. It sounded like thunder rolling up and down Mt. Olympus.

Apollo had seen this many times before, and he knew that his best course of action would be to let things run their course. Even Hera smiled as she watched her husband lose control. On the other side of the coin, she had also seen him lose it many times when he was angry, so she would take this six days to Sunday. But it was time to get down to cases because besides Apollo's story, they still had to tackle the prophecy, which needed to be addressed and resolved at least to some degree. She was about to get back to business when, to her surprise, Zeus stopped himself.

"Sorry, it's been a long day, and this was just what I needed," he said sincerely. His broad grin was genuine. "Go ahead, son."

"Well, I parked behind some trees and ran in to see what I could do. I had her free in a jiffy. I had to shift a rock over a bit, and she was good to go. And she was SO grateful that she offered to—"

Zeus turned three shades of white and got a sickly look on his face. He shuddered as he imagined what it was she had offered!

"You're not going to sit there and tell me that the two of you--?"

Caught by surprise, Apollo quickly got his father's intimation and answered with a sharp and resounding "NO! Don't even think of going there! Are you kidding?"

The King, and his Queen, let out such a big sigh of relief that a windstorm swept down the mountain.

"But you were on the right track. There is a woman involved, and Pythia, well—"

"Set you up with her?" Zeus chimed in.

"Sort of," Apollo answered.

"Say what, Pol?" Hera queried.

"She took me into the cave of time and let me see what this woman would be like in the future."

Hera was on a roll with her questions. "Wait a minute, what is wrong with' today'? Why couldn't you just see her today? And why did you have to go into the cave? She can pretty well conjure up whomever she wants; isn't that how it works?"

Remarkably, Zeus followed along with his wife's reasoning and was on the edge of his throne, waiting for the answer.

"You should see her, father—about five-three, dark hair, beautiful eyes, and an attitude that won't quit. I loved just listening to her. She is not only beautiful, but she is the smartest woman I've ever met."

Now the King was lost, and Hera wasn't far behind.

"Whoa, back up a minute, young man. I know you're excited, but you lost us. Keep it simple. OK?"

"OK, folks, shoot."

"This woman is from Sicily, but you first saw her in the cave of time, and then you went to Sicily?"

"She is from Sicily, and if Pythia had just brought up her vision for me to see, I would not have been able to talk with her and spend time with her. That's why we were in the cave. When we spoke, it was twenty years in the future, and that was in Sicily. But right now, she is still inside her mother."

Zeus and Hera looked at each other, and things began to click.

"And her name is, what did you say?" Zeus asked rhetorically.

"Maria!"

Just then, in a flurry and a flash of light, Athena showed up. "Sorry I'm late, folks. They sent the wrong soul down to Hades, and I had to fish him out of the river Styx. Quite funny, actually. So, what's going on?"

"Well," Hera said deadpan. "To paraphrase a song title from the distant future, 'how do you solve a problem like Maria'!"

CHAPTER SIXTEEN
THE ODYSSEY

Unbeknownst to the gods, Nick was also trying to solve a problem like Maria, and, unbeknownst to him, it was both different and similar. If this seems confusing hearing about it after the fact, just think about dealing with it in the present tense using a mind already cluttered with doubts and hopes and contradictory information.

Here he was trying to make a good impression on his "new friend," as one colleague referred to her, and doing just the opposite. He was apparently in dire straits because he inadvertently took "the" book of hers - *The Odyssey.* And, of course, there was his job, which admittedly he was pretty good at, but the cast of characters with whom he had to deal, and all the new administrative crap introduced made it harder every day.

Lost in his thoughts about the Sicilian and all that had happened since the opening of school, Nick forgot about the imminent faculty meeting. Luckily, he happened to look up at the clock staring down at him from its perch over his door, which reminded him not only about his obligation to get his butt in gear within the next few minutes but also clicked the philosophic switch in his mind, which, throughout his tenure on the planet, was all too easily and way too often tripped. He was in a lifelong battle with time, a battle he knew he would eventually lose, and it bothered him how it controlled every aspect of everyone's life - especially his. Of course, the meeting hanging over his head exacerbated his feelings of ill will toward anything remotely connected to being punctual, which was not very high on his list of priorities. It wasn't even on the list at all. He also did not want to be the last one there and have everyone staring at him as he walked in.

The meetings used to be held in the faculty lunchroom, which was next to the cafeteria where the students ate. This was easy and convenient: down the hall, get there early (a brownie point or two), bite his tongue so as not to get involved in all the ridiculous rhetoric spewed (which he was semi-successful at), then walked down a set of stairs to the parking lot and got out of town. But since the construction of the "Media Center," all meetings were held there. It was upstairs near the main office and a real pain in the neck to get to quickly. They had to justify its construction, the two-year disruption to the school day, and the enormous amount of money it cost to build. Nick had changed his tactics, so he would be *one* of the later half dozen or so arrivals, which meant he could sit outside the main confluence of desks and tables. That way, he didn't have to look at whoever was speaking and could more or less tune out what was going on without being too obvious. Nick grabbed his jacket and briefcase and was about to leave when he remembered Maria's book. He might as well give it back to her at the meeting and tone down any ill-will she might be conjuring up.

Nick's timing was perfect. The whole teaching staff was already there, and three or four stragglers came in after he did. He sat alone at a small table, took a sip of coffee, and started looking for Maria. She didn't seem to be in her usual spot with all the other English teachers. Where the hell was she?

"Sitting with all your friends, Nick?"

It was Jim. He was usually one of the first ones there, but today he was dead last!

"Hey, shithead. Did you oversleep, or did they let you have two for the road at the Crescent Tavern?" Nick shot back without blinking.

"Neither. You goldbrick. Just trying to get caught up with my backlog of papers. Some of us actually read the work we assign."

"Yeah, well, that's your stupidity."

Meanwhile, the meeting proceeded at full blast, and the principal seemed to look over his shoulder after Nick's last remark. Most people, of course, would have just shut up, but that wasn't Nick's M.O., and he just couldn't help himself.

"I didn't mean you, Mr. Morgan. I was speaking to my partner here."

The quizzical look on Morgan's face indicated he hadn't heard anything Pappas had said, which was pretty much what happened with anything Nick had said the entire time Pappas had been principal. Jim just shook his head as politely as he could.

"OK, that's all I have for today. Here's Bill with some details about our next set of drills." That would be Bill Grant, one of the vice principals. He was a straight shooter and all-around nice guy. He was good at his job and was one of the few administrators Nick liked, and the only speaker at the meeting Nick would actually pay attention. Jim liked him as well, but there was some problem with the mike and projector, so there was to be a couple of minute time out while the tech nerds got everything squared away.

Nick took the opportunity to look over *The Odyssey*, a book he hadn't read since college.

"What the hell are you reading?" Jim asked with feigned astonishment.

"It's *The Odyssey*, you frickin' moron," Nick shot at his buddy.

"I know what it is. I was just surprised to see you with it. Were they out of the Classic Comics edition at the library?"

"I didn't get it at the library, crap face!"

"Amazon?" Jim was laughing so hard he could barely get the word out.

"It's not mine. It's Maria's," Nick answered matter of factly.

"She gave it to you?"

"No, I took it by mistake as we left lunch duty."

Jim shook his head vigorously.

"Man, are you in deep shit!"

"Hope you're not talking to me," Bill Grant laughed as he headed back to the mike after a quick drink of water.

"No, Bill. Talking to Nick," Jim explained. "Nick, tell him whose book you took without asking!"

"What's the big deal?" Nick loudly asked. "It's Maria's."

"You're in deep shit, man," Grant said with a smile as he stepped back up to get things rolling again.

That was the third "deep shit" regarding Maria that Nick had heard within a couple of hours. Was the third time the charm? What was the deal with Maria? Was she some sort of witch? Did they know something about her that he didn't know? Nick would soon find out the answers, or at least partial, pseudo answers to these and many other uncertainties. But the problem of the moment for Nick was should he look for Maria and give her back her book or try to make a quick exit and go somewhere where he could sort things out. But that question was soon to be superseded by the call for questions from the staff, the most asinine and unnecessary part of every meeting. And they always saved it for last!

"Does anyone have any questions or concerns?" Morgan asked.

There was always at least one person who wanted some attention, and it was usually the *same* teacher whose hand went up first. Yup, Alex Weber! You could set your watch by him. Every year Nick said that he would keep track of 's total Weber's queries, but he would get so angry he never did get around to doing it. All right, let's see what we all have to sit through today, Nick thought to himself.

His first question had been answered earlier. The second one was a simple contingency "what if" that a second grader could have figured out without breaking a sweat. AND they both pertained to only his department. Nick wasn't about to give him three strikes today, and, even though saying something would lengthen the meeting further, he just couldn't control that Greek temper.

"Can't these things be done by email or in a department meeting?" he blurted out. Everyone turned to look at him, and a couple of people gave a thumbs up. The "question asker" had a big scowl on his face, and Morgan scrunched his big nose down at Nick, followed by a verbal reprimand.

Nick was contrite - for him. "OK, I didn't mean to interrupt. Sorry. But you did ask if there were any concerns, and if I want to retire in ten years, I don't want to still be at this meeting." For his part, Weber waved at the principal and said he would email him what he needed to know—meeting over, finally!

Before Nick could get his stuff together and decide on a plan of action, he glanced up to see Maria headed his way. She had that look in her eye. Well, she always had "a" look in her eye, and the problem was that Nick could never tell what it was and precisely what it meant. Not then, not now, not ever, and this is written about thirty-two hundred years and thousands of miles later. Huh? (Just keep reading...).

Jim quickly excused himself with a wink and a wave, and the rest of the staff seemed to melt away as they flowed past Nick and Maria and then vanished into the late afternoon.

"Well, I see you have MY book, Nick!"

"Yeah, I emailed you about it. I didn't mean to take it," Nick said apologetically. He started to hand it to her, but she waved him off.

"I'll tell you what, my light-fingered lunch partner - keep it overnight, and OPEN it, and see what you think," she said solemnly. And then her demeanor changed, and she added with a big smile, "Quiz tomorrow, cafeteria, period 7. And I'll give you a hint: you have something very much in common - disposition wise - with the hero. Be ready."

Nick was so dazed and confused that he didn't even watch her walk out, which was his loss. Was she serious? It looked like he was in deep shit.

CHAPTER SEVENTEEN
THE QUIZ...

Nick couldn't remember being as nervous as he was when the bell for period seven rang. Not for the college boards, or his first day teaching, even his first day in the Army. He ran down the hall to the cafeteria, only to find Maria seated, correcting papers, and ready to go to work on him next.

"Well, did you read it?"

"Not ALL of it," Nick answered defensively.

"No, not all of it, you blockhead. I just wanted you to get a feel for the hero and the entire work. It's pretty famous, you know."

"I think I might have heard of it," Nick said with a somewhat softened, sarcastic smile. They both laughed. "Was that the quiz? Just to see if I had ever heard of t it? Did you know that Odysseus' home was just about twenty miles from Cephalonia, where my parents were from?" Nick added.

"No, I didn't know that. That's interesting. But did *you* know that he landed in Sicily at least three or four times on his way back home? Some accounts have him stopping there as many as seven times!"

"Seven, are you serious?"

"Yeah, Nick. He liked it so much that he kept coming back! And there is no quiz. I just wanted to put a little pressure on you. Odysseus had a lot of pressure on him, but he fought his way through it."

"Yeah, but he didn't have to deal with you!" No sooner were the words out of his mouth than he realized that it was the worst thing he could have said. What the hell was wrong with him?

Maria cocked her head back and feigned shock and surprise.

"So, you have to 'deal' with me, huh? That must be a terrible burden. Poor boy!"

Nick knew that he was in a deep hole, as she just sat there and gave him a protracted, galvanized scowl that seemed to slice his face to pieces. He couldn't just sit there and say nothing, but what in the world could he come up with to correct his stupidity. Nick decided to take the advice he would often give his pitchers when they were in trouble: "Go soft...." And that's what he did.

"I'm sorry, Maria." That's all he said.

She broke into a big smile. "You damn Greeks are all alike. That's one of the ways you and Odysseus are very similar, you know. You both have a BIG MOUTH."

"And don't forget Ralph Kramden from *The Honeymooners*," Nick chimed in. He was still sweating profusely even though the tension had been broken. "The three of us make a pretty good trifecta, wouldn't you say?"

She rolled those beautiful eyes, and whatever she said next went right by Nick, who was captivated by her mere presence. Maria caught on to his comatose state so she repeated what she had just said. "You know how he almost blew the whole voyage cause he couldn't keep his big mouth shut, don't you?"

Nick shook his head. "OK, I'll tell you, but I want you to read it. Odysseus and his crew had just escaped from the Cyclops, and they were out of danger, but his ego came up front and center, and he couldn't resist yelling out who had blinded the giant. He shouted his name so that the heavens themselves could hear it. Of course, the Cyclops did not appreciate being the fall guy, and he hurled half his island at the sailors, killing everyone but Odysseus."

"What an idiot," Nick said while he shook his head.

"Sort of like someone who just couldn't let the faculty meeting end. He had to get his two cents in."

"You mean the science teacher who always asks the questions?

"I mean YOU!"

Nick could see why she was such a good teacher. She sucked him right in. And she was right!

"Lotta good lessons in here, Nick," Maria continued as she tapped a finger on the book. "Lotta good stuff!!"

Nick couldn't resist his next statement, but he thought he would throw out a disclaimer first, "I know you don't like cliches, Maria, but this one fits. You're not just another pretty face!"

"I bet you tell that to all the girls," Maria countered with a smile a mile wide.

"I think that could be considered a cliche - touché!"

She was still smiling, but her head shook a mile a minute. "Just read it, you hardheaded Greek. Oh, and here, you might like this one as well," she said as she handed him another book. "This is for you; you don't have to swipe it as you did *The Odyssey*."

He couldn't resist an appropriate *Honeymooners* line. "You're a riot, Maria, a regular riot. Thank you very much…really."

It was *Meditations* by Marcus Aurelius.

He was floored. Either Maria wanted to be nice and just share some of these famous thoughts with him, or she thought he was a total moron who had never read anything in his life. For the last few years, he had hardly read a thing, I mean nothing. Could she have known that? Did he give away his stupidity? He was lost in his thoughts…again.

"Hey," she called out. You might want to start with page XLI of the introduction. "Got it?"

"Yeah, yeah…OK. Thanks again."

CHAPTER EIGHTEEN
MUSINGS

When he got home, Nick did something he had not done in a long time. He just sat and thought. Not about his lesson plans, what he needed from the store, how much money he had left, or anything having to do with everyday concerns, if you will.

What started him thinking was that passage Maria "suggested" Nick read first in the Aurelius book. He sat on his deck with a thermos of coffee... no music, no distractions, and read it, and it knocked him on his ass.

> *Keep in mind how fast things pass by....*
> *Existence flows past us like a river....*
> *Nothing is stable...past and future gapes before us--*
> *A chasm whose depths we cannot see.*

Holy smokes. This frickin' emperor knew what he was talking about, and he expressed all the feelings about time Nick had grappled with his entire life. Wow! He spent the next two hours reading *Meditations,* followed by an hour with Odysseus and his travels. It was eye-opening. Nick felt exhilarated, mentally alert, and eager for more. This was all Maria's handiwork. No wonder she was such a good teacher. There was something almost mystical about her and how she went about things - always thinking, perceptive, and step ahead. Best teacher in the school...

the best teacher he had ever seen. Of course, Nick had a clumsy - at best - way of giving her her due, and he knew he often embarrassed her when he praised her in front of students or other teachers. She wound trot out her old standby when he told her privately, "Flattery will get you nowhere." Of course, he didn't want to get "anywhere" cause sitting next to her and talking with her had quickly become his favorite activity.

He took a sip of coffee and glanced at the copy of *The Odyssey* on the table. The events in the story took place somewhere around three thousand years ago, yet the names and ideas are still used today. "Helen Of Troy" had become "The" phrase for the most beautiful woman ever, and just about everyone knows what a TROJAN HORSE was (and watch out for those 'Greeks bearing gifts"). The concept of an "ODYSSEY" has been used in conversations, literature, and song lyrics - it's even the name of a car model….and the title of a "new book"! Pretty good staying power!

Nick knew all these things, but he had brushed them aside along with many other aspects of thought and philosophy that he used to pay attention to. And wasn't it ironic that the story's hero was from Ithaca, the island closest to the island where his parents had been born (Cephalonia or its modern spelling...Kefalonia). And with Maria's heritage from Sicily - how can you beat an island trifecta like that? Could all this be merely a coincidence? That is a good question. He put his foot upon the next chair, and as he tried to take a sip of coffee, he knocked his thermos over. Luckily it didn't get smashed cause he liked drinking from it. It had been given to him by a former student and bore the name of her school in large letters across its middle - a name he had not noticed until this very moment: ITHACA.

CHAPTER NINETEEN
ATHENA

The three of them filled Athena in on what had transpired with Poseidon and Pythia and the "prophecy." Still, it was Hera who did most of the narration, which was fortunate because Zeus kept getting his facts mixed up, and Apollo saw everything from the perspective of his youthful listings.

"So, that's where we are with this right now, Athena. Do you have any questions?" Hera asked as she took a sip of black coffee to ease her parched throat after the long explanation.

Athena, the goddess of wisdom, showed why she deserved that title as she cut right to the chase.

"Something is missing."

"No shit, sis," Apollo chimed in.

"No, you moron," she retorted to her brother as she smacked him on the forehead. "What I mean is, what you've told me is interesting, and would make a good story, but the possible changes to the world, if there are two beauties instead of one, don't seem drastic enough to get worked up over. There has to be something else."

Zeus could hardly contain his exuberance. He had been the king of the gods ever since he could remember, but he wasn't even "hitting his weight" with regard to being right. Zeus had been told that many times, and though he finally was able to grasp the baseball analogy, he resented the comparison. This time, though, he felt that he had hit one out of the park, and he said so.

"See, I was right. There is something else. Something else."

Apollo gave him a "high five," and Hera had to admit that her "lesser half" was, for once, on the right side of history.

The three of them looked at each other and then at Athena, who was about to ruin the King's day.

"Well, there's only one thing to do. We have to go to the source. We gotta go back to Delphi."

Wherever you were at this time, whether you had already been born or not, or if you had already lived your life and were gone, there is one thing for certain: you felt the geological disturbance caused when Zeus' jaw dropped. And it's always tough to see a grown "god" cry.

CHAPTER TWENTY
THE CAVE OF TIME

They decided to take the fast way to Delphi since speed was important, and they wanted to get to the bottom of this dilemma as quickly as possible. At first, Zeus said Apollo should not go with them as punishment for messing up the deal with Triandos, the wine rep, but he didn't want to miss the chance of seeing Maria again, and he "whined" and carried on like a two-year-old. Finally, Zeus gave into them. Who said tantrums don't work? Hera did say, though, that he might be handy to have along since he was the only one who had interrelated with this unborn Sicilian.

So, they were off with a big gust of wind and a loud thunderclap. They landed quietly in Delphi and caught Pythia by surprise, as she was sitting on an old tree stump and looked like she had just gotten out of bed. Something appeared to be on fire - dangling out of her mouth, and she was about to take a gulp from the bottle in her hand. Written on the dark bottle in some foreign tongue were the words JACK DANIELS. Zeus could not contain his pleasure at seeing her in this ragged condition, and his smirk and subsequent laughter were a sight to behold.

Pythia, however, was not amused. "Shut up, you big bag of wind, before I call every insect within a hundred miles to have lunch on your face. Didn't I tell you never to come here unannounced?"

The Oracle didn't even notice the other three heavenly visitors in her zealous haste to chastise her number one nemesis. When Hera started to speak, Pythia was so startled she dropped the bottle of bourbon directly onto her bad toe.

Of course, this resulted in another round of guffaws from Zeus, and it was only Athena's quick wits saved him from a pack of vultures summoned by Pythia.

"Please forgive my father. This was my fault. He wanted to let you know we were coming, but I felt that the quicker we got here, the quicker we would be out of your way, and we know how busy you are!"

Pythis waved off the vultures and eased up on her tirade. Her demeanor slowly shifted into that of a more gracious host. She didn't particularly like Athena either, but she was somewhat afraid of her. Athena was the smartest individual in the universe. Her powers were not diminished in the least at Delphi or anywhere else, and when things got tough…well, the old saying about blood being thicker than bile would always apply.

The "hostess" bit her lip and forced an obviously phony smile. "Well, it's nice to see you all. How may I be of service?"

Wisely, Hera decided to take over and fill her cousin in. For her part, Pythia offered refreshments, but everyone politely declined to drink out of the rather grungy-looking bottle. Apollo said he would like to try one of the "small burning torches," as he put it, but Athena smacked his hand as he reached to take one from Pythia.

"Not good for you, you big dope. They stunt your growth!" she warned. Normally Apollo would have shot something back at his sister, but his main purpose was to get some face time with Maria, and he didn't want to mess that up.

"OK, here it is," the queen of the gods began. Hera could be succinct when she wanted to, and this seemed like a good time to lay out "just the facts." When she finished, Pythia shook her head and wondered out loud what they needed from her -

"Looks like you got it all" were her exact words.

Zeus was about to blow his top when Athena put a finger to her lips and stated, politely but firmly: "There has to be something else…." She touched her thumb to her ear while she spoke, which Athena often did while either thinking or when she was about to start some cataclysmic destruction. Pythia knew when to back off.

"Oh, I see. You want the end game, the final result, the big thing that ties this all together. Am I right?" The Oracle was spot on with her succinct analysis.

They nodded, but as they were about to get the skinny on what would happen, their conversation was interrupted by a distant yet distinct echo. The echo, which resounded up and down the valley several times, faded and returned. It was disgusting to listen to, for it seemed to be someone throwing up - no, more like someone puking his guts out.

"What in the hell was that?" Apollo grimaced as his face became somewhat like a corkscrew.

"Ehhhh," was all Athena could say.

"Yes, it is what I call the midday puke. I will tell you about it when the time is right," Pythia said with a malevolent, devious smile. "But that's a story for another day. Let's get back to the business at hand."

"Let's do that, dear," her cousin stated matter of factly.

"All right. I would be happy to help, but this may take a while because there are two steps I need to go through, and it's a bit risky bringing so many into the Cave, and sometimes its predictions are affected. We are, after all, talking about possibilities and probabilities, not certainties! So, I need everyone to cooperate. Everyone…!"

She looked over at Zeus, wearing a forced grin, and gave a reluctant nod. "All right, then. Let me prepare things," Pythia said with a tone of authority.

To make herself more appealing to the eye, Pythia turned away from her guests, threw her head back, and started running her hands through her hair. She reached into the fold of her gown and pulled out a silver object about the size of a bullet. Pythia seemed to be rubbing it on her lips. She took one more swig from the bottle, rinsed her mouth with some liquid from a smaller vessel that somehow manifested itself, and spat the foul-smelling substance onto the ground. Transformed, she turned around to face her guests. Even Zeus had to admit she looked somewhat more presentable - attractive almost.

The new and improved Oracle turned to Hera and asked in a severe tone: "If I use an analogy, do you think the big guy will get it?"

"Hmm, that depends. He's usually better if you give it straight, but he surprises me on occasion. Give it a shot."

Luckily Zeus didn't hear a word of what the two women had just said. He focused on the sky to see if any other airborne adversaries had been unleashed.

"OK, here goes," Pythia uttered as she cocked her head slightly and snapped her fingers crisply in the proximity of the king's nose.

"Oh, mighty omnipotent and omniscient ruler of all the worlds - may I ask you a question?"

Now, say what you will about Zeus. He wasn't as stupid as some people (read "Pythia") thought. Not that he knew what those two adjectives meant, mind you, but he realized that at least she wasn't calling him some of the vile names she often did, so he decided to take the high road and be polite.

"Of course, my most gracious and lovely host."

Hera and Athena rolled their laughing eyes at each other, and Apollo was pinching his thigh to keep from grinning. For her part, Pythia was pretty much lost in her plan of action and took the comment from the king at face value.

"Good! Here's the question--if you spit into the ocean, what impact would that have on the state of things?"

Zeus didn't hesitate with his response, "What ocean?"

"What difference does it make? Any ocean," she responded with a scowl.

"It makes a big difference. Some oceans are usually quiet and peaceful, others are prone to storms. And is it high tide or low tide? Is 'Pol here pulling the sun across the sky, or is the moon out? Are there ships on it? If so, how many?"

Pythia shook her head. Why was she born with such power? She regretted trying to appeal to the king's higher mental faculties, if he even had them, but now it was too late. A glance from Hera told her she had to stay on the track she was on, as frustrating as that might be.

"My mistake for leaving out the details. It is noontime, it is sunny, the water is peaceful, and there are no ships in sight. Oh, and it is the Mediterranean. Good enough?"

Zeus realized he had her in a mental bind, which had never happened before in all their dealings, so he decided to play it out for all it was worth. Those two women could wait. "Well, technically, it's the Mediterranean *Sea*, not the Mediterranean *Ocean*, dear lady."

"My mistake, your highness. Of course, you are correct. If you spit into the Mediterranean *Sea*, is what I should have said. Please forgive me!" She was no dope and figured she might as well play the same game.

"You are forgiven. But one further question. When you said 'YOU,' were you referring specifically to me, Zeus, the King of The Gods, or was it a generic you, referencing any Tom, Dick, or Harry?"

Everyone, particularly the Oracle, was floored that Zeus used an expression that wouldn't be in vogue for over three thousand years, and so with a slight nod, she decided to get back to business. She was afraid that if she hit another volley, it would go on and on until the girls were born.

But Zeus was on a roll and not quite ready to throw in the towel... "Because if you're talking about the average guy, spitting into the Mediterranean won't do a thing, but if I were to spit it in, well...watch out. And of course...."

A swift kick to his shins, courtesy of his wife, brought him up short. "I was just sayin'," he pleaded with an innocent look and a wistful smile.

"May I continue? If 'someone' were to spit into a large body of water, it would be caught up with all the rest of the liquids, and not much, if anything, would change. Even if you threw a rock into the sea, it would have little effect - assuming you didn't hit anyone. But, throw a rock into the water by our side, and a series of ripples would result, getting larger and larger." She demonstrated this by firing a stone into the small pond next to the group and counting the ripples one, two, and three.

"Yes, yes, very nice. And may I say you have a good arm - for a girl," Zeus chided.

The Oracle ignored him and continued. "Now, try and follow my explanation. While a stone in the pond causes an immediate and pronounced visible impact, the ripples vanish and do not go any further than the pond's edge. Yet, if someone were to "spit" in the pond, it could be carried out by the flow into the stream, or perhaps combine with other droplets of water, and potentially cause a big change much further down in the water chain."

"Got it!" Zeus exclaimed, and he did. He was pretty good with physical cause and effect, like belting someone in the mouth or, as was the case here, the flow of water in a stream.

"Good boy!" Pythia proclaimed, and she meant it. "Now, the future is the same way. A big change will produce immediate, visible results, easy to see and measure, like a war or an assassination. And yet often, a subtle, hardly noticeable change can cause more substantial long-term effects. Got it?"

Zeus vigorously nodded as he envisioned the threat of a punch in the mouth which often had a more profound impact than actually hitting someone. He was two for two and couldn't help a bit of self-congratulation.

"All right, then. We are ready to see what the future might be - possibly."

CHAPTER TWENTY - ONE
POEMS AND PREDICTIONS....

Pythia's demeanor changed as she took on an air of seriousness and mysticism. "So, here's what you need to always keep in the front of your mind: Time is the most mysterious concept known to exist, or not exist for that matter. Some events will happen only if certain other events precede them, some *might* happen, and others will occur no matter what. BUT...all of this could change. Remember that...always remember that. Understand?"

"In other words, you don't have the slightest idea of what's going to happen," Zeus interjected as he threw up his hands and shook his head so hard that one of the bugs from that morning came buzzing out. He was back to his insolent self.

"Let's not be rude, dear," Hera snipped.

"It's OK, cuz the big lug is close with what he said, but he left out a couple of words. 'For sure.' I can't tell you FOR SURE what will happen, but I can outline the possibilities and probabilities. Is everyone ready?"

Each of them *was* ready but differently. Hera was calm and collected, Apollo was excited, Athena was contemplative, and Zeus, well, Zeus was Zeus; skeptical, puzzled, and mostly clueless. But, he *was* the king, and he did his best to show a regal countenance.

"OK, let's go," he commanded as he pointed his finger forward.

"Well, dear, we can't go in just yet."

Apollo appeared confused. Well, after all, he was the son of Zeus. When he had gone in with Pythia, there were no stops or detours, but he didn't want to appear rude.

"We can't go into the Cave Of Time just yet because this is not a one-and-done viewing, as it was with you, my young and over-sexed friend," Pythia explained as she rolled her eyes toward Apollo.

Apollo blushed such a deep shade of red the others had to shield their eyes. Zeus laughed as he slapped his son on the back; the ladies smiled, and the enormity of what they were about to do softened somewhat.

"We are going so far into the future that the powers which will be unfolding are pushed to their ultimate extreme, and we will be dealing with two of the most powerful concepts ever known to man or gods: "TIME" and "IF."

Pythia seemed to enter still another dimension as she began her explanation, and the tone of her words and the intensity of her eyes were hard to describe. Even Zeus was mesmerized, and Athena locked her eyes straight ahead as she began to absorb and contemplate what the Oracle was saying mentally.

"First of all, the Cave Of Time was not meant to hold more than three people per session. We must give it a moment or two to reflect on what it may show us and the effect of such a large number of beings on their journey through the future. Follow me, but stay several paces behind me. Do not, under any circumstances, touch any of the people in this party or anything in the cave."

No one said a word as Pythia led them along a winding, somewhat circular path along the edge of the woods, further and further and further down until she suddenly turned and abruptly put up her hand for them to stop. There was a strange aura in the air that none of the "visitors" had ever experienced before, something like the purple hue of twilight mixed in with a cloud that was thick with a smog-like heaviness and yet at the same time light and invisible. A sweet, almost honey-like aroma filled their senses, and the feeling was mystical and mysterious as the gods tried to make sense of what was about to happen.

Pythia spoke in a whisper and indicated with a finger to her lips that she was the only one to speak. Ahead they could see a large opening in the foliage, and a luminescent glow began to flow towards them - more like a liquid than the apparent mist it appeared to be.

"The cave is almost ready. After this, I will be the only one speaking unless the powers of the universe indicate otherwise. And, to anticipate your questions, there will be no doubt about when and if this permission is given. And, just so you know, 'Pol, as I indicated, what we did was different from what we are about to do. And, lest you become confused, your highness, what you saw this morning was merely a snapshot of a moment in the continuum. What we are about to explore is a different dimension. Is that clear to you all?" All the while, the Oracle's voice was dropping deeper and deeper into an almost trancelike state, and her eyes were somewhere else. It was eerie and chilling.

Apollo nodded his head to indicate that he got the message. Hera was her usual calm, patient self, and Athena was intrigued. Zeus was scared half out of his mind. This was creepy beyond belief. Battles, women, even the wine rep - those were things he could deal with. But he knew it was his job to set a good example, so wetting himself was not an option, nor was biting off half his tongue, which seemed imminent.

As they approached the opening, the Oracle bowed her head and, in a solemn tone, asked permission to enter for the purpose of the utmost importance for the smooth progression of the years of eternity. This sent chills down the king's spine, and he had half a mind to call it quits, find the wine rep, and get blown away, leaving this all in his wake, which was probably a bad choice of words.

Pythia signaled for them to follow her in single file, which they did, Athena, the inquisitive one first, and Zeus bringing up the rear. Once they were all in, there was an abrasive, crunching sound, as if someone were rolling rocks across a field of stones. At least that's what it sounded like to Zeus, who was closest to the source of the loud, grating disturbance. Zeus reflexively turned around to see what was causing all the racket and saw to his horror that a huge stone slab was making its way across the entrance. Trapped! He looked to Pythia for reassurance, but not only didn't he find words to allay his fears, but he also couldn't find her. Suddenly he felt two sharp raps on the back of his head and heard someone say: "Knock, knock."

He turned to find the leader of this trek standing right behind him, so close he could sense the blood running through her veins and feel the warmth of her skin, which was pretty ironic since his blood had turned cold, and his skin was crawling with clammy sweat. He was about to let out a yell for the ages, but she almost kindly put her finger to his lips and smiled.

"Whenever my journey into the future is as the leader of a large and diverse group, I must put the last member to the test. And you have done very well, your highness." She said that he almost liked her with such sincerity and deference, well, almost. "I told you at the outset that this was a two-step process. We have taken the first step. Now let us see what the years will hold as they unfold. Come!"

She beckoned them to follow, and all at once, the whole atmosphere changed dramatically and drastically. When they had entered, the cave was, well, a cave. Dark and damp and dank and cold. Now there were flashes of light at different times and in different directions. It was as if they had been transported into the middle of a stroboscopic light from three thousand years into the future. There were faces and places on the walls and overhead - some familiar, others unknown. There were words - poetry and songs and epithets, spoken and written on the walls and then disappearing just as quickly as they had manifested themselves. And sounds, all kinds of sounds. Laughter, rain, crying, screams, thunder, wind, some sort of whirring noises they had never heard before. Smells?

Oh, there were smells. Food, cut grass, perfume, fresh excrement, pine trees, and smoke. It was overwhelming.

Through this array of "everything," Pythia kept her composure and was as steady as a rock. She motioned for them to join her in what appeared to be a large cavern with a high ceiling and a soft, radiant light chasing away the darkness. There was room for all of them, and she motioned for her guests to sit down, which was the best news Zeus had heard in a long, long time, as he crashed his butt south with a loud thud and a rather bellicose "whew."

This drew a "look" from the Oracle, but she let it slide. They were where they needed to be, and it was merely a matter of being patient while the future mechanisms decided when to make their appearance. Their forbearance was rewarded quickly and rather suddenly, as images and voices made their presence known. But this was different from what they had experienced when they first entered. Soft, subtle, hushed.... whispers, not screams...transparent images...floating in and out of sight...the apparent appearance of a galaxy of stars on the ceiling. It was thrilling and awe-inspiring and a bit "spooky" as well, as sights never seen before and words never spoken were seen and heard and then were gone. Their heads were spinning, and their senses were peppered as they had never been before.

The Oracle broke their hushed silence with some measured, welcome words. "You may observe, listen, breathe and speak to me or each other quietly. You must try to remember your experiences here, for you may take nothing with you, and once we leave, we may not return. Ever. Please look at the sand in the vessel at the center of this opening." She pointed to what appeared to be an extremely large hourglass. "Once the last grain has been deposited on the bottom vessel, our visit here will be ended." She did not ask for questions, for none were needed.

Everyone's attention suddenly shifted from their host to the image of a beautiful woman, fair of skin and breathtaking to behold.

"It's Helen!" Zeus shouted. "Helen of Troy!" They were in his ballpark now, and he was excited to be in the know. Apollo took note as well: "She's beautiful. Not as good as Maria, though...."

There was no time to debate as a cascade of faces and objects and events poured into and swirled around the group gathered in the now crowded cavern. There were warriors, ships, forts, and what looked like the statue of a horse. This followed a sighting of an older, bearded man who seemed to be telling a story to a crowd of people intently listening. This was followed by images of temples, theaters, and sporting events. Then a whirring cloud of eclectic sights and sounds appeared with faces and places from what appeared to be different eras of what was yet to come. Then, as if someone had snapped a finger, it all disappeared in a fine mist, and there was nothing.

"But what about Maria?" Apollo enunciated what they all were thinking.

"Funny you should ask," Pythia replied with a chuckle to lighten things up.

Almost at once, the sound of some strange music began. It was nothing like any of them had heard before, yet it was pleasing to listen to and relaxing for the soul. As the song played on, an image began to come out of nowhere, and as it began to take shape, it became apparent that it was a person, a woman, about five feet three inches, with dark hair, a seductive shape, and eyes to die for. It was Maria, almost twenty years old, just as Zeus had seen her and Apollo had spoken with her. Then, in a sudden mist of a whirlwind, she turned, and an image of an older but just as beautiful woman appeared. She was seated at a table, looking into some metal device, and wearing a stylish brown outfit with leather boots - very becoming indeed - but something very foreign to the gods. Next to her was an average-looking man who appeared to be a bit older than she was. He also was peering into some device, and the two of them were laughing as they talked about something or someone they called "der Fuhrer."

"Maria?" father and son questioned at the same time.

The lady in question was stunning, to be sure, but was this the same woman, just at a different stage of her life? The man with her kept calling her "Maria;" she referred to him as Nick.

Just as everyone realized what was happening, the music softened, and words began to float through the air. Slowly and deliberately, they landed on the cave wall right near the hourglass, line by line.

"Look and see quickly," Pythia warned as she pointed to the glass, then up to the message. The sand had almost run out, and the words seemed to form some poem.

TRAVELS EAST, JOURNEYS WEST
20 YEARS WILL BE THE TEST
IN THE FUTURE...

As the poem was inscribed, another image appeared, all in shades of black and gray. It was a heavy-set man with some kind of uniform on; he was just coming in a doorway and taking off his hat and was about to say something.

And then, as the last grain of sand hit was about to hit the pile at the bottom, there was one more image; Maria stood with a Greek warrior. Then it was all gone, and they were outside the cave, dusting themselves off and trying to figure everything out.

"The poem," Zeus moaned. "That was a key. And we didn't have enough time to read it all!"

"Speak for yourself, Pop," proclaimed Athena with a big smile. "I got it all right up here!" she pointed to her head!

"But what's the story with Maria? Why was she young and then so old? Then she was young again, right at the end. And what was she wearing? And who was that with her?" Apollo was brimming over with questions.

"There were two people with her," Hera reminded them.

"Yes, two people," Apollo whined with just a touch of jealousy. "But where was I?"

Zeus started to chuckle. "You're a chip off my old block, Pol. She was with a soldier in the last image - probably a bodyguard. And earlier, we looked at what she will look like when she's older. And the clothes are probably what she would be wearing in the future if the future was not here. And 'Pol, I wouldn't be too concerned about that person sitting with her. He didn't impress me at all. Probably some sort of servant, maybe even a court jester. What did she call him? Nick? Don't make me laugh."

Then there was that brief glimpse of the third man, the rotund one... who the hell was he?

"But where would this be? And when?" Apollo was puzzled again. Yup, a real chip off the old block, all right. "The poem, Athena, what did it say? And who was that warrior with her? A guard? The poem, the poem!"

"Keep your shirt on, Bro," Athena scowled at Apollo. Here it is," the goddess of wisdom began, and everyone, including the Oracle, was fixed on every word:

> *Travels east, journeys west*
> *20 years will be the test*
> *In the future plainly see*
> *What Maria's role will be*
> *Odysseus' blood inside the man*
> *Who'll play the hero in this plan*
> *To complete the prophecy*
> *And love this girl from Sicily.*
> *BUT BEFORE THE TIME IS THROUGH*
> *THERE ARE THREE THINGS THAT THEY MUST DO*
> *TASKS COMPLETED PROPERLY*
> *THE THIRD ONE FINISHED SECRETLY.*
> *AND GIVEN OUT UNSELFISHLY....*

"Athena, you're sure that was it?"

"Positive, Hera. Word for word."

"But what the heck does it mean? Who is Odysseus? What journey? What exactly is the prophecy? What tasks must they complete?" Zeus could have easily rattled off another hundred questions, but the Oracle put her finger to her lips.

"That's what you have to find out!" She said with a quiet but resonating voice. "That's what you have to find out--and then do something about--if you can."

CHAPTER TWENTY-TWO
AFTER THE CAVE

The gods were tired, stressed, and more than a little confused. They decided to take a break, just as mortals do, and go to the beach to sit and sip and sort things out. And what better beach could there be than the one in the Aegean Sea at Santorini, known as Atlantis in those days. It was one of the wonders of the ancient world, but they weren't interested in the thriving metropolis, just the sand, the surf, and the stars. Apollo couldn't go, of course, because there was the deal made with the wine guy about the twenty straight sunny days, and the god of the sun was more than a little upset. But a promise was a promise, and, as it turned out, it was fortunate that he did not join the group. Zeus told his boy not to worry, that he would keep his interests in mind and fill him in on everything they discussed.

The island was a beautiful place, then and now. Of course, it is about half the size that it used to be, thanks to unforeseen events which would come to pass over the next few days, but we are putting the volcano before the gods, as it were. Zeus, Hera, and Athena stretched out on the beautiful, seemingly endless sand and listened to the waves lap the shore. The king decided to clear his head by taking a quick plunge into the Aegean Sea, and though the water was cooler than it looked at the first leap, it had its desired effect as he came out refreshed and good to go. He was smart enough to pass the baton to his better half, who showed she was even smarter by asking Athena to assess the situation.

"Well, one thing is certain; there are not enough pieces for us to complete this puzzle, or there are too many" Hera nodded, but her husband got that "not a clue" look on his face.

"Huh?" was the best he could do, and that just about summed it up for the king of the gods.

"OK, dad, here's what I'm saying. Maybe something not in the poem or presented during our stay in the cave would be necessary to figure this whole thing out. Or, maybe we don't need *all* the things we saw and heard, including the poem, to make sense of this."

Athena could see that Zeus was still perplexed, so she decided to try a different route to his mind. The three things Zeus was best at were consumption of food and drink, women, and some kind of confrontation, verbal or physical. She decided to avoid the middle one and throw him somewhat of a curve combining the other two.

"OK, so, father, you are having a gathering of your friends and business acquaintances, and you are playing 'find the wine,' which I know you are very good at."

Zeus perked up his ears. They were in his ballpark now.

"So, if I remember correctly, each team is given seven clues, and the one who finds the wine first gets to drink it. Am I close?"

"On the money, Honey," Zeus quickly replied.

"And, while you have to be able to find the prize using the list you were given, aren't several of the items intended to throw you off?"

"YES!" Hera jumped in. "The key to the game is deciding which hints to follow, and which to disregard!"

For once, the king of the gods seemed to be on top of things!

"So, you think that that is the case here. Yeah, yeah, I never did trust that damn Pythia!"

Hera took exception to the potshot at her cousin and pointed out that the Oracle did not control what they saw. She was merely the guide.

"And remember, this is all at best speculation. No one knows the future for sure."

"Ladies, I bow to your reasoning and logic. So-- what's the next step?"

"I think the key to this is people - not only the people in the poem but others, like the images we saw in the cave and the things they represent. AND, we have to determine what the prophecy involves, and when it is supposed to occur."

Athena pointed out that Helen of Troy seemed to be at the heart of things, even though she was not explicitly mentioned in the poem. Perhaps they shouldn't dismiss Maria's future companion as sappy as he looked. She had called him "Nick," so he could be Greek and might just be as important as the warrior they saw her with as the sand was running out in the cave. And, of course, there was Maria herself, who was the centerpiece of this whole puzzle.

This was a lot of thinking for one day, even for Athena, so Hera suggested that they get some food and wine and watch the stars come out over this beautiful island. There would be time tomorrow to figure things out. Or so they thought...

CHAPTER TWENTY-THREE
HAS ANYBODY SEEN MY ISLAND?

"I'm not snoring, Hera. Go back to sleep," Zeus pleaded as he felt his wife trying to rouse him with what seemed like sledgehammers disguised as her fists.

"GET UP. WAKE UP. GET UP!" Hera pleaded.

"Make up your—"

Zeus didn't get to finish his sentence, as some supernatural force seemed to turn everything upside down and inside out. The surprised gods were lifted into the air and dumped unceremoniously back to the ground with a series of thuds-- one, two, three, four.

Dawn was breaking - literally. The volcano had taken leave of its senses and was spewing fire, rock, and anything else it could get out of its belly. The normally calm Aegean Sea began hurling wave after wave crashing onto the shore, and the ground seemed as if it were giving birth to another world as quake followed quake.

Even though Zeus was the king of the gods, certain things were beyond his capabilities. This was one of them, and the three of them knew it. It was all they could do to keep their limbs attached to the rest of their bodies as half the island came crashing down into the sea. There wasn't much they could do to help the people; it was essentially every citizen for themselves. They would have to put all their immediate concerns on hold as they struggled to get out in one piece and re-convene at a new location to assess the impact of this calamity. They were set to make their exit when Athena casually mentioned that dealing with the prophecy would have to be put off, and Maria's fate would have to wait.

"Maria," Zeus exclaimed as he turned to face Athena. He had forgotten all about her, and this quick reminder caused a momentary lack of focus that wiped out the sight of the boulder speeding toward his head. Bang! Thud! Splitting headache.

"Are you all right?" Hera asked fearfully.

Her husband shook the cobwebs from his head as he answered, "Yes, Maria."

"How are your eyes, Dad?" Athena asked worriedly.

Zeus turned to face the goddess of wisdom, but he was dazed and out of touch with their predicament. "My eyes, Maria? 20/20."

A quick flash of lightning shot through the group as the three of them made their way out of the crumbling city. Hera looked at Athena as they grabbed Zeus by the elbows and headed skyward.

"Did you hear what I think I heard, 'Thena?" Hera asked in dismay

"I'm afraid so," Athena answered. "I'm afraid so. Your husband just sent Maria three thousand years into the future!"

CHAPTER TWENTY-THREE
AND A HALF
PICKING UP THE PIECES

The three of them made their way to Mykonos, an island near what was left of Atlantis. They seemed alright physically - they were, after all, gods - but mentally and emotionally, they were worn out. There was a trip to the future in the Time Cave. The puzzle of what was to be and what might be, the catapulting of the Sicilian, as they came to call Maria, about three thousand years into the future, and now, to top it off, the destruction of one of the premier civilizations in the world.

They knew that rebuilding the city and helping the citizens would be their first order of business. Athena suggested that she do a flyover to scout the damage and to help decide what the best ways to help might be.

CHAPTER TWENTY-FOUR
OH, WHAT A SURPRISE

It was rare that Pythia hosted a gathering of the gods. Not one of them could ever remember her giving out even a crumb of food or a sip of wine. To top it off, her partner was Poseidon, whose home in the depths of the seas was a ready-made excuse for being the guest at many an affair but the host at none. But there they were, at Delphi, Pythia, and Poseidon, with a ton of food, barrels of wine, and even music (courtesy of a rather talented harp player), just waiting for the invitees to show up. Athena was the first to arrive, followed by Apollo. The two young gods helped themselves to some bread, cheese, and olives, as the Oracle and the god of the sea were toasting each other.

"It's so generous of you to have this gathering for us," Athena said politely.

"Yeah, I was looking for something to do tonight, and this hit the spot," Apollo enthusiastically managed to say through a mouthful of crusty bread soaked with olive oil. "Good eats! Thanks!"

"Well, we figured we owed it to you, especially your father, and it's been a while since we all got together," Poseidon offered with a wry grin and eyes as wide as the ocean. "Where is he?"

"Right here, 'Bro, right here." It was Zeus and Hera. "I heard what you said, and we do appreciate it. It's nice to get together and see, uh, everyone." The king couldn't resist casting a disparaging glance at Pythia, but a quick knee to his shin from his wife brought a forced smile back to his mug.

Poseidon was wearing a coast-to-coast smile, which was rare for him because of his usually sour personality and the toll being underwater so much would have on even the most jovial of beings. He certainly didn't fit into that category. But today, he was like a stand-up comedian prepping for his set.

"So, older brother, how have things been," he asked Zeus in between bites of food, in this case, spanakopita (spinach pie) and feta cheese, washed down with some Sicilian red wine. It was a considerable amount of wine, followed by another large tumbler or two.

"Well, we had a close call at Atlantis, but things are getting back to normal little by little. Did I see you in the distance while all this was going on? You didn't perhaps have a hand in that catastrophe, did you, little Bro?"

At first, Poseidon thought he might try to appear hurt by this question of his humanity, and even though he knew Zeus wouldn't buy it, after some quick consideration, he decided it would be fun anyway.

"Come on, man, have you ever known me to create havoc like that? I had nothing against that island or its people, and I watched just to be sure you were all right."

Zeus could have recited many instances when Poseidon lost his temper and caused monumental damage to man and beast, flora and fauna. Still, it would have been foolish to bring them up now when things appeared to be rolling along reasonably smoothly. Plus, the food and drink were delicious, and since he and Hera were guests, there would be nothing to clean up! You couldn't beat that with a stick, as Apollo always said.

Pythia had been unusually quiet all this time, but the inscrutable look on her face let everyone know that she had at least one card up her sleeve, and she played it with a smile, which was also unusual.

"I hope everyone is enjoying their repast. I can't tell you how wonderful it is to see you all here seemingly without a care in the world, now that the Maria episode has been put to bed - if you'll pardon the expression."

Hera started to reply, but the Oracle cut her off and continued, egged on by the god of the sea, who raised his cup high and added a hearty "hear, hear." And the reason I can't tell you how wonderful it is is that 'Seidon and I need to come clean on something, right dear?"

"Right, honey!"

Zeus didn't miss the terms of endearment, and it was all he could do to swallow the huge wad of cheese in his mouth without choking. He hoped they were spoken just to aggravate him and were not for real, but either way, he decided the repast was too good to blow by losing his temper. Zeus would, for once, be cordial and courteous. It would soon prove much more difficult than he imagined!

Pythia continued, smiling all the while! "Why doesn't everyone help themselves to some more food and drink, and then we will present our little surprise, all right?"

Food and drink were magic words to Zeus, so he helped himself. He wondered what precisely the surprise was, but first things first. Wine, bread, cheese, olives: all present and accounted. Main course: pastichio, spinach pie, legs of lamb. Baklava and koulouria for dessert plus all the wine you could drink. What could be better?

While Zeus and Apollo were stuffing their faces, Pythia and Poseidon were rolling out a cart with a large, clear, round structure at its center. Hera and Athena lowered their wine glasses and looked intently at this strange object, and even the father and son eating team seemed to pause and reflect on this thing - whatever it was.

The god of the sea and the oracle had been chomping at the bit to get to this part of the evening because nothing could contain their enthusiasm. Poseidon started it off: "Ladies and gentleman, and my brother, I present for your enjoyment and entertainment, the one, the only. love of my life - PYTHIA – master of all things seen and unseen."

As he introduced her, he raised his right arm, and a wave landed at the feet of the guests, brushing against their feet as they watched in awe. Even Zeus was impressed as he bowed his head to acknowledge his brother's showmanship, "love of my life" comment notwithstanding.

Pythia spun around three times, her almost sheer gowns flowing in the breeze. She stopped right next to the object, curtsied delicately, and ran her hand around the circumference of this "thing," being careful not to touch it.

"What is that, Pythia?" Athena wondered with a puzzled expression on her pretty face.

"Yes, please tell us," Hera added with urgency in her voice. "We are dying to know what it is….and what it does!"

"It's called a Crystal Ball. I found it in the cave when I was cleaning it out. Women with special powers will use it in the future to tell fortunes. It's almost like a portable Cave of Time."

Athena was confused. "You found it in the Cave of Time? You mean other people use it as well? I thought it was just yours to use wherever you choose."

Pythia felt that this might be a good point to give her guests some additional background information so she wouldn't have to explain everything over and over again as she was doing her "presentation." Though with Zeus there, that wish might be impossible to realize. She had to explain it to Poseidon three times, which was one-on-one. Well, it would be worth a shot.

"I will give you a quick lesson on the Cave of Time and time itself; it's a bit hard to follow, so if you all could refrain from stuffing your stomachs and focus, I will give you the skinny on all this, no pun intended. Everyone stopped swallowing and turned to face the Oracle. Everyone, that is, except Zeus, went merrily along with gorging himself.

Pythia turned toward him wearing a scowl that would have stopped a shooting star and frozen it in space. "AHEM, your highness—"

The king wiped his mouth clean and took a quick gulp of wine. "Oh, I'm sorry. Did you mean stop eating right now?"

She turned with a disgusted look on her face and began as if nothing had happened. "The first thing you must realize is that time is an illusion. There is no such thing as the past or the future." Everyone, except Zeus, wore a perplexed look. "You'll have to take my word on this because the full explanation would take days--and in some cases - (as she looked at Zeus) - a lifetime."

Normally the king would have been upset by such a slur, but he was still trying to figure out how time could *be* an illusion, which was fortunate as it turned out – since it was that much less for him to roll around his brain.

"The Cave of Time allows access to different corridors of happenings, which may or may not come to pass, and it is open to all those who possess the knowledge of how to access its secrets. In other words, people in the know can see what it might show, from those who lived many years before us to those in the distant years to come. Are we good so far?"

Hera, Athena, and Apollo nodded hesitantly, while Zeus raised his fist high in the air to signify a vehement yes. Truthfully, he didn't know what she was saying, but he reasoned that the quicker she finished her tutoring session, the faster they could all get back to the goodies staring up at him.

"This particular tool of the trade, as it were, is almost like a mini, portable cave in that it can show things unavailable with just our senses. I happened to find it covered with dust in a remote section of the cavern, and since no one answered my lost items call, it is ours. I am going to show you a brief glimpse of what people would watch from their homes on a thing called 'television.' It is not as good as the Greek plays, but for what it is, it isn't bad. Watch!"

With that, she rubbed both hands on the top of the crystal ball, waved her cape with a flourish, and a figure appeared on the globe. He was rather rotund and had on what seemed to be some sort of uniform - but it didn't look like a military uniform. He was coming in the door, waved his hand, and exclaimed, "Oh, what a surprise!"

Hera and Athena immediately recognized the man as the same one they had seen during their time in the cave. So did Apollo. The king was very interested but, at first, didn't make the connection, so he did the logical thing, he asked the Oracle who that was.

"His name is Kramden, and his job is to carry people from one place to another on a chariot-like contraption called a bus. He and his friend, and their wives, get into all kinds of humorous situations - somewhat like the way you do, your highness."

"So, it is for amusement. He is funny to look at. Why does he say what he does? And does this have something to do with us, and what happened to Maria?"

Zeus continued. He was on somewhat of a roll, and he thought he might as well ride the hot hand. "And you're about to tell us what this all means! Am I correct?"

Poseidon gave him a thumbs-up and was just about to continue with the background to what they were about to see when two new guests made their appearance. It was Aphrodite and Triandos, the wine man.

"Hmm, I don't recall inviting you, 'Dite," Pythia offered.

Poseidon, who was generally on the sour side, jumped in to keep the festive feeling going 'cause he sensed that this partner was about to upset the applecart, as it were.

"Well, you know it had to be an oversight. A thousand apologies. Please join us. We have plenty to eat and drink, and the more friends here, the better. Sit and eat."

Triandos didn't have to be asked twice. He grabbed a goblet of red wine and a large chunk of bread dripping with olive oil. Zeus looked at him in disgust as he wiped the oil from his chin and, all in the same motion, shoved a piece of feta into his mouth. Aphrodite was content with some white wine and a few figs.

Pythia, who you would never accuse of having a suitable "bedside manner," drew her lips into somewhat of a snarl as she looked around to see if there were any other interruptions. Zeus wanted to get things rolling as quickly as possible. He couldn't deal with *this* woman scorned, so he interjected as diplomatically as his ego could stand, "Please continue, dear Pythia. We are anxious to see what you have to show us."

"All right then," she began. "As I was saying, what you are about to see is a glimpse of what mortals will be looking at thousands of years in the future. It is called television. TV for short."

Pythia waved her hands above the crystal ball, and the image of a comedian appeared. She snapped her fingers, and his image froze.

"We saw this guy in the cave, right?" Apollo yelled excitedly.

"Correct, nephew," Poseidon said. "Very observant."

"Look at the expression on his face. What would you call it?" Pythia asked.

"Stupidity!" Zeus shouted.

The Oracle's eyes rolled almost onto her cheeks.

"I think what we're going for is 'surprise,'" Hera said softly.

"Or 'confusion,'" Athena added.

"Yes! Yes! A double play, ladies!" Pythia exulted. "Right on! Now, look at this scene and tell me what you think."

The celebrity faded out and was replaced by several men who seemed to revel in inflicting bodily harm on the others. They were kicking, slapping, punching, and knocking their heads together. And then they did it all over again!

The gods went crazy with laughter, with Zeus leading the way.

"That was great," he began. "But they must be hurt badly," he managed to say between his guffaws and knee-slapping.

"It's all fake, man, it's all fake," Poseidon explained between his spurts of laughter. "It's all fake."

"You're kidding!" Apollo gasped in wonder. "Wow!"

"Well, this was entertaining, my dear hosts. Why was the first man in the cave, and why are we watching this, to begin with? Am I missing something?" Zeus asked candidly.

This inquiry, which was sound in its intent, brought a grin to the Oracle and a big smile to Poseidon. He took it upon himself, with a nod from his partner," to explain things to his brother, which gave him a great joy since, for once, he appeared to know more than Zeus did.

"Here's the deal, Bro. These things show that nothing is certain. We saw a look of surprise and confusion on the man's face. He was in the cave to remind us how life is…both in the future yet to come, and in the past."

"And the other guys showed that what we see is not always what is?" Zeus added.

Everyone's head turned with a genuine look of admiration for the king that he had not seen in a long time. He had nailed it, and he was justifiably beaming just a bit.

"It shows that we, both mortals AND GODS, often jump to the wrong conclusion. NO ONE is infallible," Athena added, with a sideways glance at Triandos, who gave her a quick wink in return. No one else noticed either unspoken signal, which was probably just as well since there was a lot to absorb besides the wine, and there was more to come.

Poseidon looked at Pythia to see if he should resume his narrative. She nodded, and he was off to the races. "Bro, do you remember a while ago when you had me convinced that the sea would go dry, and you had me running around like crazy trying to get water and avoid the destruction that would follow? Remember that?"

Zeus not only remembered, but it had been one of his favorite practical jokes ever, and he broke into a big smile. "Yeah, man, I had you going."

"It wasn't so funny from my side of the water. I got so stressed my hair started to fall out."

The king could barely contain himself as he pictured his brother half hairless.

"Good memories, huh?" Pythia asked. "Now, does this blast from the past ring a bell? You came to my place of business - it was about six months ago - mid-morning, hungover and still pretty much drunk as a skunk. Remember?"

Now, Zeus had had countless hangovers and truthfully could not recall this one. He shrugged honestly. Pythia continued with her narrative disregarding the interruption.

"—and then you puked your guts out right near the entrance to Delphi. It was so long and loud that the echo has still not faded."

"That's what we heard the night we entered the cave," Athena shouted.

"Uh, huh, you got it, sweetie."

Zeus started to recall the incident and slowly nodded.

"Starting to come back to you, huh, big guy? Well, that has cost me a lot of business. I can't tell you how many pilgrims got turned off by that sound (not to mention the rotten egg smell, which still permeates that whole area) and just turned around and walked away. What do you have to say for yourself?"

"I'm sorry" was the best Zeus could do. He sort of meant it, too.

Poseidon and Pythia embraced and then stood there, interlocking arms and smiling. Zeus downed two goblets of wine, one white, one red, in the blink of an eye. Either that, or he lost his lunch in front of the crowd.

The two "P's" spoke together, which prompted two more wines for the king. "So, dear king of all there is, we figured we owed you one. Or actually, two, as it were. Are you ready?"

Zeus was half in the bag, but he figured the worst was over, so he nodded reluctantly. Pythia passed her hand over the ball, and who should appear but Maria and the one she kept calling Nick. Apollo jumped up. "Maria!" He effused excitedly.

"You have your father's keen intelligence," Pythia observed sarcastically. It was indeed Maria sitting at a table with Nick. The two of them were looking at something in those in those boxes each had. They were laughing hysterically, and while it was unclear what they were watching, the words "der Fuehrer's face" seemed to be repeating. With each chorus, the two burst into new gales of laughter.

"Didn't we see something similar in the cave?" Hera observed.

"Yes," said Poseidon, and "No," proclaimed the Oracle.

Puzzled looks all around - except for Aphrodite and Triandos. Now it was Pythia's and Poseidon's turn to laugh, laugh, and laugh. They high-fived each other and then laughed some more.

"You want to tell them, or shall I?" Pythia asked the god of the sea.

"You go ahead, dear. It was all your idea," Poseidon joyfully responded.

"OK, that works for me." Pythia turned to face Zeus directly, and in as dignified and formal a voice as she could muster, she began. "Well, your majesty, 'Seidon and I figured we owed you a big one for what you had done to us. So, we put our heads together, rigged some things in the cave, and voilà - we brought Maria, or more precisely her image, three thousand years back in time and made you think she would be a potential rival to Helen of Troy."

"And you fell for it hook, line, and sinker, as we say in the depths," Poseidon snickered. "Hook, line, and sinker."

"Yes, we made you THINK, THINK, and THINK some more. Ha ha ha…we knew that would be a terrible ordeal for you! Worse than hornets, even. And, by the way, they did that on their own. They were not thrilled by that vomiting episode either!"

Hera and Athena were unsure what Pytha meant, and they asked for some clarification. "Do you mean to say that Maria is not from Sicily and is not still waiting to be born?" Hera asked. "Is that what you're saying?"

Poseidon took up the explanation. "Oh, she's from Sicily, all right, but she won't be born for another three thousand years, give or take."

"So, she could not possibly be a rival for the most beautiful woman in the world!" Athena reasoned.

"No, not in this century. And let me say, we were sorry we had to get to the three of you involved to the degree that you were," the Oracle continued as she waved her hand at Hera, Athena, and Apollo, "especially you, my young buck. But when you saved me that day, I figured that your visit with Maria would be another piece your father would have to consider. Please forgive me."

Apollo shrugged his shoulders and hinted that perhaps she could find him another woman when she got a chance. Pythia gave him a big hug.

"And we had no idea what would happen at Santorini," Poseidon added.

"We were going to tell you the next morning - only there wasn't the next morning."

If there was one thing Zeus understood, it was revenge, and he had to admit that his brother and Pythia had run a pretty slick scam. He was normally not a good loser, but he had been on the other side enough to appreciate artistry when he saw it, even if it was at his expense.

"So, the two of you staged the whole thing. Pretty slick, Bro, pretty slick. And you were your normal devious self, my dear Pythia. I would have expected nothing less! We are in the presence of greatness. A toast all around now that we are even, and everything is back to where it should be." Zeus bowed deeply three times and then took a huge gulp of wine. He was sincere, and they all took a deep swallow.

"Just one question - where did that poem come from? Athena asked. "It was well written and intriguing, to say the least."

Poseidon and Pythia pointed at each other, then did a double-take. "I thought you wrote it, you eloquent sexpot," said the god of the sea.

"—and I thought you were the poet," she retorted.

Zeus couldn't stand it any longer, as he looked Pythia square in the eye and proclaimed: "If you thought my brother had the talent to write something as good as that poem, then you're dumber than he and I put together."

That brought the house down with some earth-shaking bouts of laughter – except for Aphrodite and Triandos, who merely smiled.

"Something tells me there is more to this story, and the two of you could fill in the blanks, as it were?" Hera stared with a knowing look on her face.

"Yeah, Sis, we're all dying to hear what you got," said Apollo with a grin. "Let's have it!"

Aphrodite looked at Triandos, who nodded and waved her on. "Ladies first, my love!"

"All right, but let me say at the start that it was my partner who found all these things out, and it is quite a story. And I know how some of you hate cliches," as she looked at Athena, "but a picture is worth a thousand words." She produced a stack of laptops and gave one to each onlooker as she spoke. "These will be known as laptops. I 'borrowed' them when I visited Maria and Nick."

With Triandos' help, the goddess of beauty showed them how to open the devices and turn them on. A scene appeared, showing a mountainous, lush region with hundreds of beautiful grapevines reflecting the late afternoon sun. It could have been any one of several areas in the Mediterranean, but this pristine location happened to be in Sicily. Taking up the narration, Triandos indicated as such. They filled the guests in on the region and its produce, which, in this area of the island, was predominantly red wine, barrels of which were being enjoyed by the gods as they watched.

"Now, this is probably the best red wine in the whole Mediterranean area, and the competition among the growers is fierce. Sometimes it gets out of hand." Having introduced the scene, Triandos pressed a button, and suddenly, about a dozen men appeared on horseback, with large swords in their hands. They rode with abandon through the vineyards, slashing and trashing as they shouted epithets while destroying most of the grapes. They left as quickly as they had arrived. They never noticed the little girl crouched in the hollow of an old log just past the edge of the grapes. She was about ten years old, with black hair and a dark complexion.

"Who is that?" Athena inquired.

"That is Maria's great grandmother - also named Maria. She witnessed the whole thing, which was done by a rival family trying to corner the wine market by destroying this family's means of producing the drink of the gods," Triandos went on to explain that this sometimes happened because of the win at all cost mentality of some of the growers.

"Very interesting," Athena remarked. "So, Maria is here?"

"No, but she would have been had we not stepped in," Aphrodite said. "Why don't you fill them in, Vasilie? You can be more succinct than I am."

"Sure. Now, this happened fairly recently. Look at your screens."

They all did, and what they saw was the little girl explaining what she had seen to her parents, who then went to the heads of the other families to plan some sort of retaliation against those who had pillaged the vineyards. But as long as she remained in Sicily, the little girl would be in danger - even when she grew up - for bearing witness against the vandals.

"So, when I told Aphrodite what happened, we decided the best thing to do would be to get her and her family out of here, geographically and metaphysically." He could see the puzzled looks on the faces of Zeus and Apollo, so Triandos answered their question before it was asked. "We sent them to the future, to a different time, and to a place that won't be discovered for over twenty-five hundred years. A place called New Jersey."

Hera and Athena got it right away and nodded as they processed all that had been revealed. Zeus and Apollo were blown away by all they saw and uttered an almost simultaneous "wow," which pretty much summed things up.

"The ironic thing is that people who want to hide where and when she is now often come to Sicily. Her trip was just the opposite."

"What about the poem? And the prophecy? Is there one?"

"Ah, yes, there's a prophecy, and the poem is an interesting tale in and of itself. Would you like us to continue?" the goddess of good looks asked.

"You bet your ass," Zeus blurted out. He quickly apologized for his earthy comment, but he had expressed everyone's feelings, albeit rather vulgarly.

"All right, you asked for it," Triandos commented. "Get some more food and drink, fasten your seatbelts, and watch your screens. I will let the young lady fill you in since she did all the legwork on this."

"Thank you, sir," Aphrodite began, "but my partner is too modest. He's the one who knows what's happening wine-wise, and most of the strategy and tactics have his fingerprints all over them."

Zeus turned his head toward Apollo and whispered, "I bet that's not all he has his fingerprints all over!"

Aphrodite did what most daughters do and ignored her father. "What you are about to see is three trips back to the future interwoven with an excursion to the near future. Things will become clearer as we view the screens if you keep in mind that since we took Maria's family out of their element, so to speak, we had to be sure their place in 20th Century Jersey would be somewhere they could successfully make their home. They all looked at their screens as the picture of the TV show faded out, and a new, familiar one emerged - Maria and Nick seated where they worked, but it was from a different angle and showed several hundred young people in the same room. They were sitting at a series of round tables, and most of them appeared to be eating and talking. From time to time, one or two would come up to Nick or Maria and then leave for a few moments and then return.

"What's going on?" Apollo wondered.

Aphrodite filled them in. "This is the school where they teach. They are now in what they call lunch duty, where they have to supervise the students while they're eating. The students who are leaving will relieve themselves and will come back shortly. Let's watch and listen a bit."

The scene narrowed to focus on the two teachers. Often the students would stop to talk with them, and there was quite a bit of laughter. Several of the boys walked up to sign out to use the toilet. They had been in Nick's class that day, and they all liked to kid around with each other.

"Hey, Mr. Pappas, that was a pretty good class today," a guy named Jack exclaimed. "I liked it."

"Thanks for telling me. I had been worried all morning that it hadn't been up to your standards. Just sign and get out. We have people waiting!" Nick deadpanned.

The boys walked out laughing and shaking their heads. The boys were replaced by three young ladies who started to talk with Maria, or, as they called her, Ms. Orlando or Ms. O.

"Did you grade our papers yet, Ms. O?" Jeannie asked.

"You just turned them in last period," Maria shot back. There was a lot of give and take between the two of them and all sorts of students who came and went during the next thirty minutes or so.

"They seem to be popular with the students," Athena interjected.

"They are that," 'Dite confirmed. "They are both good teachers and treat everyone fairly. Let's see what they say to each other."

"Well, Nick, did you read some more of The Odyssey? What did you learn from it?"

"Believe it or not, I spent most of the night looking through it. The last time I read it was in college, and Homer hadn't quite finished it yet."

"Had he even started it?"

They both laughed. Nick was a bit older than Maria, which she kidded him about quite often and which he used as a self-effacing jab at himself.

"You're really into this, aren't you, Maria?"

"There's a lot to be learned from this tale. What did you learn? What's your favorite part?"

"Well, you gotta give Odysseus credit for his persistence. Ten years is a long time to travel the distance he did. Of course, there were a lot of obstacles in his way, and he did spend seven years with that nymph in the cave - what was her name, Calypso?"

"Very good, Greek! She must have made an impression on you! You have to

remember that she had him under a spell and even offered him immortality."

"Yeah, well, seven years is still a long time. You can't tell me that he couldn't have escaped if he had wanted to. Now, it would have been different if you had been back there with him - he might never have left!"

"You're terrible," Maria countered with a smile.

"They seem to get along pretty well," Hera observed. "And he appears to be a decent man."

"Yes, he is a good guy, although he has his moments, which you will see. He likes to joke around with the students, and especially with Maria! He keeps complimenting her on her appearance and will tell anyone who listens that she is the best teacher in the school, which aggravates her - even though she *is* the best teacher in the school."

Aphrodite went on to explain the prophecy and how it was Triandos who stumbled onto it once they had decided to put Maria's family into the safety of "witness protection" in the future. But the main protagonists, including Maria, had to be checked out thoroughly, and the exact meaning of the prophecy was not precisely the way it was written. That had to be investigated as well.

"Why don't we all watch for a while? You can get the feel of what's happening. Remember, even though this is the future, the things you see have already happened."

That's fine with the ladies. As long as there was food and drink, Apollo and Zeus were in as well--let's all grab a seat and watch along with the gods.

CHAPTER TWENTY-FIVE
A TRIP TO SICILY

Where the heck was he? Jim, DW, Lefty, and the other teachers from his department were all sitting at desks and writing away like there was no tomorrow. Wait. He looked over at the next row, and a flock of English teachers did the same. They were all busy as hell and writing away like there was no tomorrow! No computers, just pens and paper, and the desks were more like plain old small tables rather than desks. Something wasn't right. These two departments met together once in a blue moon - the last time had been over ten years ago when the Middle States evaluation team was about to come through to certify that the school was all it was supposed to be. Did they still even have that? Secondly, although Nick did enjoy the "view," since several comely females taught English, where was Maria? It was like the '27 Yankees without Babe Ruth!

He looked down at his workspace, and apparently, he had been laboring at some sort of essay himself. The title was "What Am I Doing Here," which was what he was wondering. He couldn't remember writing it or even starting it. And why was he writing an essay in the first place? He figured he might as well read it. Maybe it would give him a clue to what in blazes was going on. Let's see, "what am I doing here?" He started to go through it, and it was not too bad a concept, as it began as a metaphor for existence as a whole and wended its way back to this meeting. "Not bad, if I do say so myself," Nick said more or less *to* himself.

While he was patting himself on the back several of the other teachers were bringing their work up to what looked like a long counter in the front of the room, and someone dressed in some sort of uniform appeared to be checking on their work. What was this, a quiz or a new requirement for the teaching staff? "You can't make this stuff up," he thought quietly to himself, remembering one of the favorite sayings of a former colleague.

He couldn't quite see the person, but whoever it was, she was diminutive in size and very expressive in her comments, and he could see her hands weaving a rhapsody as she spoke. There was something very familiar about her. Holy shit, it was Maria!

"Yes, Jim, excellent job. Just give me a good conclusion, and you've got your A," he heard her say to his friend from across the hall. An "A" that didn't sound like the Maria he knew. He remembered her marking the essays from her class during lunch duty, and there was usually more red ink from her marking pen than blue ink from what the students had written. Several other teachers brought up their work and came away smiling, with nice comments echoing as they left, so he figured he'd take what he had written so far and get his share of the compliments.

"Hi, Maria," he said with a smile.

She seemed rather cold and almost unfriendly, but he had seen that side of her before, so he didn't think much of it as he handed her his paper. He started to walk back to his desk, as some others had done, but she waved her hand to indicate that he should stay where he was. A frown filled her face, and she started shaking her head as her pen crisscrossed his paper.

"You can do better, Nick. Much better. Go back and start this over."

He was about to say something but thought better of it. Maria looked as if she were in no mood to be crossed, although as he glanced back, he could see her smiling effusively at Janet Ryan, another English teacher.

"Very nice, Janet. Interesting to read and tight and pithy. You deserve the 'A' I'm giving you." He had read some of Ryan's work, and it was consistently good, so he just put his head down, determined to get on her good side, grade-wise. Several history teachers appeared to be done as they took their papers up to the "fastest pen in the East," as he had called her one day during lunch to signify her alacrity when correcting papers. He thought to himself; she should like this new beginning as he dashed off a couple of paragraphs and took his work back up.

All his colleagues seemed to be getting nothing but compliments, and he was confident that he would hear the same thing this time. As he was walking up to the counter, he noticed what Maria was wearing. He always noticed what she was wearing, and he could probably recite her outfits as well as she could, but he had never seen this one before. It was a blue charcoal color, a very official looking skirt and jacket, with pins on it. She looked like an airline pilot. Lost in his thoughts, Nick neglected to take note of his location, and he walked right into the podium, which had somehow appeared at the center of the counter. At least this time, Maria seemed to be smiling - or was she laughing?

She reached over the podium as Nick just stood there, somewhat in a stupor. "Well?" She asked. If nothing else, Maria was a master of short utterances. "Lemme see what you got?"

Nick was just returning from his trip to his unconscious - or was it his subconscious? "Huh?" was the best he could do.

"Your paper, nut head, lemme see your essay!"

"Oh, oh, here it is." Nick handed his paper over the counter and crossed his fingers.

Maria took a glance and shook her head. "Strike two," was all she said as she handed it back to him.

"But everyone else is getting an 'A,' why don't I?"

"Everyone else deserves an 'A,'" she countered.

With his tail between his legs and no idea how to proceed, Nick slunk back to his desk, detesting his fellow teachers and not thrilled with the person running this travesty of a meeting.   Suddenly, everything, and I mean everything, changed. The back wall, which was hinged, opened up in a sweeping roll toward the outside to reveal--wait--it looked like an airport? What? And right in the forefront was a large jet, a 727 perhaps? The company's logo was painted in large letters along the jet's side with OLYMPIC AIRWAYS, essentially the national airline of Greece. Were they still in business? He turned to his left to get a reaction from Jim, but he was gone. In fact, all the teachers were gone except for him and Maria. She was wearing a broad smile, and he could see a mischievous sparkle in those beautiful eyes as she walked toward him and took his arm.

"Let's go, man. They're waiting for us."

Nick didn't know who was waiting, why they were waiting, or anything else. All he knew was that he was arm and arm with a beautiful, smiling, voluptuous woman, and, as a bonus, he didn't have to finish his essay.

"NICK! NICK!" The words were uttered simultaneously with an elbow into his rib cage.

"I'll change the essay. I'll change it—" he half screamed in surprise. "What's the matter?" He looked up and found that he was in the cafeteria, to his astonishment. What the hell?

"Just a heads up that Morgan just came in the far door. You had that 'thoughtful,' spaced-out look about you, and I didn't think you wanted him to see you thinking," she said with a grin.

"I wasn't asleep, was I?"

"No. I would have woken you up right away. I can't take the chance that he'll fire you. You think I want to do this by myself? You had that faraway look in your eyes, so tell me. Was she good-looking?"

"Yes, she was, 'she' was you. You were running a class, and then this plane...oh, hey Brad, what's up?"

"Couple things," the principal began, without an attempt at any kind of greeting. "First of all, it might be a good idea if the two of you didn't stay here the whole period. Maybe take a walk around, or even sit at opposite ends of the cafeteria. Just to keep everything and everyone covered. Know what I mean?"

After the battle over his essay, Nick was in no mood for any crap from anyone, especially this jerk. Luckily, though, he composed himself before speaking, and Maria did a double-take as she listened to his calm and courteous reply. "You're absolutely right, Mr. Morgan. And I think we've got it covered. One of us takes a walk around the room every ten minutes so the students know that we know what's going on. But we feel it would be better for both of us to have this location as a base, as it were, to more properly monitor the girl's and boy's rooms, which are right outside this door. Does that make sense?"

The principal was stunned and speechless. All he could manage was a lame "OK" as he turned and walked silently out the door.

Maria gave Nick a resounding high five and a big smile. "Wow, Nick. That was awesome. Do you think you could keep your daydreams at bay while I run to my room?"

Nick nodded and cocked his head with a smile. "Yeah, yeah…I'll try to keep them under control. Take your time."

Maria made her exit with Nick's eyes riveted on her silhouette as she disappeared into the hall. Just as the door to the cafeteria was closing, an announcement came over the speakers.

"Ms. Orlando, please report to the Main Office. Ms. Orlando, to the office, please. Thank you."

Nick wondered why they wanted her; the principal had just been here. No sooner had he gotten his question formulated than the door reopened, and Maria walked back in, shaking her head as she sat down.

"One of these days, they'll get their act together here - hopefully before I retire. I ran into Morgan in the hall, and he said they wanted O'Connell in the office, not Orlando."

"I thought you were going to your room?" Nick wondered.

"I wanted to get a book for you, but it turns out I had it with me."

"Well, where is it?" Nick demanded.

"Will give it to you at the end of the period. Get some work done," Maria kidded. "Lemme know when there are five minutes left. You'll like it."

He knew better than arguing with her, and he did have many papers to grade - as did she. Of course, Maria always had a lot of papers to grade, but this was the first time she told him to get busy. Maybe he was too much of a pain today? Nah, no more than any other day. There was something not quite kosher, but he couldn't put his finger on it. Luckily, as it turned out, he couldn't put his finger on it to be more than a bit crass. As Maria would always throw at him, "You said it, I didn't." Then it hit him, her leg. Whenever Maria had a skirt on, she would cross her legs under the table, and the top portion would go back and forth a mile a minute. He noticed it by chance the second day of lunch duty, looked away, and never looked back again (believe it or not). It was the ultimate test of his willpower - but he could tell when she was doing it because she *always* did it, and secondly, the table would vibrate just a bit. But, today, there was a skirt, but no leg. Hmm, what was up?

The more he got to know Maria as the days drifted by, the more he was convinced there was something almost mystical about her. She must have read every book ever written, and while that was an obvious hyperbole, it wasn't that far from the truth. She could quote from Socrates, Mark Twain, Shakespeare... and it seemed as if she could recite *The Odyssey* by heart. Maria knew more about sports than most of the men in the business; she liked all kinds of music and had seen just about all the great movies ever made. There didn't seem to be anything that she wasn't well versed in. Nick used to kid her that she was one of the Greek gods. Today that didn't seem to be a joke. Something was definitely out of place.

But then, the more he thought about it, the more unsure he became. He had been wrong about Maria's mood before. He had been wrong more often than not. Maybe she was just tired. Other than that - well, he could never really figure her out. Who was he to judge, anyway? He thought he'd better play it close to the vest - not his strong suit by any means.

"What's the matter, Nick? You seem a bit out of synch."

"No, I'm OK. How about you, are you doin' OK?"

"Just fine. And you know something? You're a good guy, and you're so kind to ask about me. I have to drop something off at Sally's room. You alright on your own again?" she asked with a smile.

"No problem. Do what you have to do."

Maria walked out in less than ten minutes for the second time, and Nick couldn't have been more confused. That is, till about two minutes later when she came right back. "Confused" didn't come close to describing the state of his bewilderment. He made Zeus look like Einstein. As for playing it close to the vest, Nick was about to put all his cards on the table.

"Thanks, Nick. Didn't mean to be so long. Did you miss me?"

"I always miss you, Maria. You know I can't live without you and that I think about you every minute." Holy smokes, what was wrong with him? Much, I'm afraid. He had just spilled his guts and waited for the ax to fall. But instead of hell, he got laughter. She was laughing. Whew. Wait, that was funny to her?

"You're a piece of work, Nick. You always make me laugh, or scowl, or throw my hands up in exasperation...or all three at once."

For once in his life, Nick left things as they were, more or less. "Yes, I have many talents, don't!" he concluded with a smirk.

Maria shook her head lightly and smiled. "You don't happen to have a marker with you, do you? Any color will do, Nick."

"Sure, gotta have a bunch in here. Gimme a second." Nick bent over to pick up his case, but it wasn't there. Nor was he "there." He was sitting on an Olympic Airlines jet, and Maria fastened his seat belt. There were no other passengers on the plane.

"Lemme just buckle up for takeoff, and I'll be back once we're airborne," she said with a big smile. Was Maria a flight attendant? He was back-- well, back wherever he had been? What happened to the cafeteria? What happened to his mind? What happened to reality? Not that he minded being with Maria on a plane headed to wherever, but he also didn't want to lose his job. As far as he could tell, teaching in High School was reality. Or was it? Maybe he was in another dimension, or at the very least in some other world.

His thoughts were interrupted by the sound of jet engines getting louder and louder. The plane was moving and very soon started its ascent, heading for God knows where.

"Hello, ladies and gentlemen, this is your pilot speaking. Welcome aboard Olympic flight 2020, non-stop to Sicily. I will give you the particulars once we reach cruising altitude. In the meantime, sit back and enjoy your flight. Your flight attendants will be by shortly to get your drink and food orders." The pilot's voice was very familiar - "hello, hello?"

"Holy shit," Nick whispered to himself. "Holy shit, holy shit, holy shit." He must have repeated it a hundred times. This was not hyperbole, to reuse a term that had become an everyday part of the vocabulary courtesy of his cafeteria co-conspirator, as Maria used to refer to herself. She would use the "h-word," as it came to be known, every time Nick seemed to be exceeding the realm of reality with his comments, and even when he wasn't, at least from his perspective. He closed his eyes, hoping that things would make sense - at least a little when he opened them again.

He fell asleep, and Rip Van Winkle had nothing on his nap, he thought to himself. As he awoke, Nick thought he heard a sound, not unlike that of the ocean lapping softly onto the shore, and he seemed to sense the smell of saltwater. That's it. He was crazy, and there was no doubt about it.

CHAPTER TWENTY-SIX
TIME TO CHOOSE

"Hey Greek, you want some lotion? Sun's pretty hot here." Nick looked up to see his lunch duty partner, but they sure as hell weren't at lunch duty or anywhere else in the school. Maria sure as hell wasn't wearing a dress. The dress was a fashionable one-piece, dark blue bathing suit. She looked sultry and stunning as the sun bathed her shoulders in a radiant gossamer-like light. The light cascaded perfectly over her dark hair with a vibrant, radiant glow. As far as he could tell, they were on a beach. He could feel the sand between his toes and hear the ocean lapping onto the shore. The smell of the salt in the air and the coconut sunblock on Maria brought back memories from days too long ago to count and conjured up possibilities of what might lie ahead. He started to wonder where they were but then mentally slapped himself. What difference did it make? He was in paradise with a beautiful woman. There was only one possible explanation. He had died and gone to Heaven.

"Do you have any idea where you are, Nick?"

"On a beach?"

"Wow, you're as sharp as ever. Very good," Maria laughed good-naturedly. "We're in Sicily. Don't you remember what the pilot said? Sicily is where I'm from, man. Do you like it?"

"It's breathtaking!" Nick exclaimed. And it was. Pristine white sand, clear, blue-green water, the sun just starting its ascent into the

Mediterranean sky. "No wonder Odysseus didn't want to leave this place!'

"Of course, word on the street is that his companion was ultra-hot, and they pretty much spent all their time in the cave. But, as you said, he probably could have escaped if he wanted to," Maria added.

"Well, lemme say this. I'll take you six days to Sunday over her - sight unseen."

"Yeah, yeah." Maria smiled.

"I know you're really into all this Odyssey stuff, more than anyone I know, teacher or otherwise. How come?"

Maria answered his question with a question of her own, which was often her M.O.

"Think about it. You rock-headed Greek. It's a 20-year adventure if you throw in the war at Troy; it has heroes and villains and beautiful women; hate and lust and pride and stupidity, and it all takes place in one of the most beautiful parts of the world. Shouldn't the question be: 'Why isn't everyone onto this?'"

Well, when she was right, she was right, which was just about all of the time. She was also always about two steps ahead of Nick, with a witty comeback to everything he said. He had to dust off his brain just to try to be even close to being in the ballpark with her; he knew it, and she knew it. He told her once, or more probably several times, that besides being the best teacher he had ever seen, she was also the most remarkable person he had ever met. Everything she said about the Odyssey and its intriguing aspects was true enough, but there was still something more godlike than mortal about her. He would kid her about this quite a bit, but it wasn't just tongue in cheek in his overactive mind. It turned out that, for once, he was right.

He was shaken out of his thoughts by a double "Hey, Greek." His standard "Huh?" response came out three times, followed by a couple of "What's?"

"You wanna go test the water a bit?"

"Yeah." It normally took him one hundred words when ten would do, so singletons took Maria by surprise and Nick.

"Who am I with, Calvin Coolidge?" she kidded. "Come on."

They walked down to the water's edge. The sun lit their way, and a bevy of seagulls provided the musical accompaniment. It was an idyllic scene and also somewhat surreal. Maria walked right into the water, but Nick hesitated at its edge.

"Well? What are you waiting for?" she asked him incredulously.

"It always takes me a while to get used to the water."

Maria couldn't contain her laughter. "Hey, this isn't the Jersey shore - the water is warm. What the hell kind of Greek are you? What would Odysseus say?"

As she was speaking, she started splashing water all over the hesitant Nick, which was no mean feat considering she was laughing hysterically. He splashed back at her a few times and then wound up for what he hoped would be a tidal wave. But he slipped, caught only the top rim of the water, and wound up doing a belly whopper on his butt.

Zeus doubled over in a roar of uncontrollable laughter as he watched the screen. Luckily, it was a one-way feed, and neither Nick nor Maria could hear him. Poseidon seemed to get an even bigger kick out of it.

"You know, these Greeks have the reputation of being great sailors, but this one can't even take care of himself in shallow water. Reminds me of that overrated clown from Ithaca. Pretty good, huh, bro?" Poseidon concluded as he slapped Zeus on the back.

"Right on, man. This guy's pretty funny. And I don't even think he means to be. You say that he's gonna make this all work? This guy?"

"Yes, this guy and Maria. They're a good team," Aphrodite added. "If you've been watching, you should have picked up on a couple of things. And if you've missed something, just keep watching!"

"You're all wet, Nick - ha, ha. Let's get you some sun."

"Sounds good to me, Maria. What a clutz I am."

Nick waited in vain for her to disagree with him, but he knew that he was a klutz in just about every imaginable way. So, he just grinned, and they made their way back up to the blankets. The sun felt good, and Maria's smile and a wink made him feel even better. He looked at the surroundings and still couldn't believe his eyes. It was like a movie set - everything was perfect - the sun, the sky, the sand, the sea...the Sicilian. What an alliteration! He turned to thank his companion for bringing him to such a great place, but it looked like she was dozing, so he cupped his hands behind his head and just took at the moment. A gentle breeze seemed to bring back memories from all over his life. He wondered if something like that might have happened to Odysseus on his famous trek around the Mediterranean. It was no wonder Maria was so enamored with this man, with this place, with this epic.

Suddenly the wind shifted and started blowing directly toward the beach. It was not gusting at all, just steady, and for some reason, the sun, which had been almost instantly overhead, seemed to drop toward the horizon. Almost like a spotlight, it illuminated the tops of the waves as they gently kissed the sand. It seemed like a Broadway show with the star about to emerge, and that's exactly what it was, but the "star" here was Aphrodite. She was like no one he had ever seen before, present company excluded, and her classic beauty was pure and breathtaking. Her hair flowed gently down across her soft shoulders, her eyes were gentle yet intense, and her smile could have warmed Valley Forge. She walked gracefully onto the beach and headed directly to Nick. Maria seemed to stir, but a wave from the goddess sent her back into a deeper slumber.

"It's nice to see you again, Nick," she began.

"Again? Again?" And then it hit him. "That was you in the cafeteria while Maria was gone. THAT WAS YOU! I thought there was something peculiar about the way she was acting. I mean, she called me a good guy."

"You know, Nick, I believe she does think you're a good guy - that's just not her way," the goddess continued. "I was trying to find out if you were who you appeared to be, and I think you are. You're perceptive and caring, and you keep your word. And, as much as we can determine, your family tree stems from a very famous Greek wanderer and warrior."

"What? For real?"

"Yeah, for real. That's why I had to check you out, to use a rather modern phrase. You have been a gentleman with Maria, and that's not easy for any guy, particularly a full-blooded Greek - and one who has his roots on an island with a connection to probably the most famous Greek of all. And, just in case you're wondering, I know all about the leg."

"Holy shit...oh, I'm sorry for the language. Just how long have you been watching me?"

"Oh, we've been watching quite a while. And don't worry - the words Zeus often uses make your expletive seem like a quote from Socrates."

Nick was in a daze trying to come to grips with this new reality. "Could we back up a bit to see if I have all this straight?" Nick wondered sincerely.

Aphrodite nodded and gave him a backhanded yes with her hand, indicating that he should proceed.

You are, I mean you are, Aphrodite, the goddess of beauty? Correct?"

Aphrodite ran her left hand down her body and did a rather seductive curtsy. "I'll let you judge."

This was too much to "face," as it were. Two gorgeous women, and at least one of them a goddess! Nick had to turn away before he said or did something to get himself into serious trouble. He gently whispered a "whew" and wiped his brow with his fingers.

"And you mean there were...are - all the gods, just like in the books?"

Aphrodite just looked at him with an expression that could mean only a resounding yes. Zeus, meanwhile, was more than a bit irate that his very existence was questioned. Still, when Hera reminded him about his grappling with everything since his initial visit to Delphi, he got a quick dose of empathy and calmed down.

Nick did have one more question of the gods, and it was a doozy. "So, am I to understand that you are interested in us because Maria and I are part of some sort of grand, orchestrated plan that impacts the universe? Some kind of fate?"

"Uh, huh. We just call it a prophecy."

Nick was getting into it, as this seemed to be right up his alley. "So, I guess it was lucky we happened to have lunch duty together, or this whole odyssey would not have taken place, right? A very ironic coincidence, wouldn't you say?"

All the gods, Aphrodite, and the ones watching on the laptops broke into gales of laughter. Nick was perplexed. What a shocker.

"Nick, there are no coincidences. While it may seem that events occur accidentally and that one piece of life is paired with another piece by chance, nothing could be further from how the universe runs. Everything happens for a reason. Got that - everything happens for a reason. It's like sewing a rug, thread by thread. The threads are put next to each other by design, and when you step back, you can see the entire picture. I'm a pretty good judge of character, and you're an upstanding man, and you're also a bright guy. I think you're getting what I'm saying, right? Most people don't understand or believe this, but you must always remember that that's the way things work."

Nick sat there with his mouth open a mile wide in astonishment and his brain in overdrive, trying to conceptualize what he was hearing. The goddess continued. "See, the universe likes things to be as neat and smooth as possible, with as few ragged edges as possible. Here's a good example. I know you and Maria are thinking of writing a book about teaching. What was your partner's name when you were writing songs all those years?"

"Mario."

"Yes, Nick, MARIO. And he was Italian as well, yes? And you never wrote with anyone else. Correct?"

Nick nodded.

"So, you take the MARIO and change the 'O' to an 'A,'" and you have?"

"MARIA," Nick gasped. "Holy crap."

"MARIO…MARIA… Just a coincidence? Please!" the queen of beauty emphasized.

"Oh, Lord." Nick exclaimed, "You mean there is a connection?"

"Nick, everything is connected, sometimes obviously, often subtly. Think about this one while you're in the groove, as they say. Who was the first woman in your life?"

"You mean my first girlfriend?"

"Jeez, no wonder Maria gets frustrated with you. Not your girlfriend, you rock-headed Cephalonian, your mother!"

"What about her?"

"She was a teacher, I believe, correct?"

"Yes, she was—"

"And her name?" the goddess continued.

"Marica."

"So, correct me if I am mistaken, but you've gone from MARICA, the English teacher, to MARIA, the English teacher - just drop the 'C.'"

Nick was floored. "You mean that's a connection as well?"

Aphrodite just looked at Nick, but he got the message.

"This is fascinating," he commented sincerely. "Fascinating and spooky."

"Yes, Nick, fascinating and crucial. Remember that the universe has to have things as seamless as possible. So, now it's up to you and Maria."

"What is?"

"What is on second," the goddess laughed. "But this is no laughing matter - it's up to you."

"Who?"

"Yes!"

Nick couldn't help but feel he had stepped into a comedy routine, but Aphrodite beat him to the punch.

"They were from Jersey, too, you know."

"Who was?"

"Abbott and Costello."

Nick broke into a belly laugh when he realized what he had said. "I was just trying to lighten things up a bit."

The goddess continued, "but I think I'm leaving the universe's fate in good hands. Understand?"

"Yes, I do," Nick said with conviction. And he did get it. He had pretty much believed this kind of thing his whole life. But Maria was another story. Would she buy into this? Or was she, as he started to suspect, part of this entire thing from the get-go? Whatever the case, he needed to talk this over with her, or, more accurately, to get her opinion since that had usually been the last word on anything they had ever discussed. He turned to get her to take on what had just happened, but she was gone. He looked back toward the goddess to find that she had departed. What the hell? Within the space of a few seconds, two women abandoned Nick. That was a new record, even for Nick.

He started to panic just a bit, and before you judge him too harshly or label him a coward, remember that he was in a strange land, by himself, and over five thousand miles from home. Luckily, he hadn't yet realized that he was also three thousand years from home. He had two choices, and he wasn't about to stay there and wait, so he started off to find his missing traveling companion. She's the one who had gotten him here, and he didn't think she would abandon him. Wait, that might have been her plan all along. He was a pain in the neck on many a day, and he did come unhinged at the slightest provocation, but was she that desperate to be rid of him that she would take him halfway around the world? That was a question he decided would be best left unanswered.

So, he just started walking away from the sea in hopes of finding a hotel or resort or at least some other people taking in the day. Strike one, strike two, strike three, you're out, Nick. He walked for close to an hour and found nothing and no one. Holy cow, what was going on? Where was he? And, as he often brought up in his sociology class - "when" was he? This could be a secluded, off-the-beaten-path hideaway not yet commercialized. But that didn't seem likely. Even in the most remote destinations for travelers, there was always some sign of the business that was running things - somewhere. And, where the hell was Maria? And that thing with "Aphrodite." Was this some sort of Hollywood trick? Some skeptics still thought they filmed the landing on the moon on a movie set. Maybe that's what this was. But why would someone go to all this trouble just to fool Nick Pappas?

And then he saw it: some kind of distinct marking in the sand, about forty feet in front of him. It looked like - it was - an arrow pointing toward a small inlet about a quarter-mile to the northeast. Who put it there, and why? Was it some kind of trap? Nick chuckled at that thought. How much more "trapped" could he possibly be? Could Maria have made it? Why here, so far from where he started? Or was it *so* far? As clueless as ever, which is saying something, he decided to go in the direction the sign pointed. As one of his friends always said: "Trust to luck." He had nothing to lose--or did he?

The gods were riveted to their screens. Zeus was like a little kid in front of the TV.

"This is exciting and puzzling. I wonder who put that arrow there and where all the people are? I feel bad for this guy. What's gonna happen to him?"

This typically "Zeusian" comment drew a knowing but very slight tilt of the head from Hera and a roar of laughter from Apollo, who seemed to have inherited his father's intellect, or, more precisely, the lack thereof. But then he, too, began to realize Nick's predicament, and he changed his tune, as it were.

"Yeah, I feel for the guy. I wish I could help him. 'Dite, why didn't you clue him in while you were there?"

"The whole point of this was to see what this guy was made of,"

Athena interjected. "That's why 'Dite took his measure a bit at the school and then set up this second test. Am I right, Sis?"

Aphrodite cordially thanked Athena for saving her the trouble of explaining, even though she was a bit peeved at her sister for interrupting something that was essentially her show. She was tired of being thought of as just another pretty face - well, really the "prettiest" face - and she wanted some credit cause she and Tiandos had put one over on everyone, including her smart-ass sister, Athena. But, since she had a couple more cards up her sleeve, she decided to let this go for now.

"Look, he's going in the direction of the sign in the sand," Zeus shouted. "Let's see what happens!"

What happened was that despite all his lifelong rhetoric of encouraging sayings and metaphors, Nick was beginning to feel the pressure, and, in a word, he was scared. The sun was well past three-quarters of the way done with its daily journey, and the current course he was on didn't seem to be offering up any answers, arrow, or no arrow. There was still no sign of another human being, and as he walked, his path seemed to be going back toward the sea, and he started to hear the water rippling onto the sand once more.

"What the hell," he reasoned. "I'll stick my head into the Mediterranean, and maybe it will knock some sense into me so I can figure out what in blazes is going on."

His plan was cut short when he saw two silhouettes standing at the edge of the sand. Yes, it looked like it was a man and a woman, and they were engaged in an animated conversation, complete with hand gestures and loud bursts of expletives - followed by what appeared to be soft, soothing entreaties on the part of the man, who was facing Nick. The woman? Maria, who else! He couldn't see her yet, but he could see the guy plain as day. He was tall and muscular and barely had any clothes on - some torn rags of what looked like it had been some sort of uniform. Somehow his image looked familiar. It was probably a good thing that he was way out of earshot because, as you should know by now, Nick wasn't good with new situations, especially when it involved someone he cared about.

Nick had missed the conversation when this "stranger" saw Maria just casually walking and called to her. She had been musing about various things and didn't hear him at first, and she was initially reluctant to talk with someone she didn't know. However, there was something familiar about him, and once the ice had been broken, she found him quite fascinating. He had been shipwrecked and wasn't sure where he had been beached.

Maria was in her usual flippant mood as she asked him who he was. "And what was your name again?"

"Odysseus. From Ithaca."

"Yeah, right. And I'm Helen of Troy."

"Well, I have seen Helen of Troy, and you are not she. But you would give her a run for her money looks-wise if I do say so."

"You damn Greeks are all alike. As I always tell Nick, flattery will get you nowhere!"

"And who is this Nick, your sweetheart?"

"No, no, nothing like that," Maria laughed.

"But he would like to be!"

"No, no, we're just friends."

"And is this Nick by any chance Greek?"

"Yes, he is," Maria answered emphatically.

"Well, if he is Greek and doesn't have any desires for you, he must be a homosexual."

She burst out laughing. "You're pretty funny, Odysseus, or whatever your name is. No, no, no. Although--now that you mention it, that would explain quite a bit. He's so up and down emotionally, and he's always worried about making me mad, and he's very knowledgeable and creative. Do you think? No, wait, he couldn't be--could he?"

While the debate about his sexual preferences waged, Nick had been getting closer to the two protagonists.

"Hey, Maria, who's your friend?" was his uncharacteristically blunt opening. "What were you trying to do, ditch me?"

"Greek, if I had wanted to ditch you - and the thought has crossed my mind a time or two - I wouldn't have brought you six thousand miles. As the old saying goes: 'I had to see a man about a horse.' Didn't you see the arrow? And, this is a fellow countryman of yours. Odysseus, this is my Nick I've been telling you about. His lineage is from Cephalonia - not too far from Ithaca, right?"

"Ah, the big island. Just a short swim from my home." Odysseus appeared impressed. The two island Greeks shook hands and then hugged. The scent of sunscreen on Nick and the smell of the sea on Odysseus made for a rather pleasant mix. As they were finishing their embrace, the purported hero of the Trojan War looked at Maria and shook his head in three or four quick movements.

"He's not. I can tell."

"I'm not what?" Nick wondered.

"For once, just leave well enough—" Maria interjected and then turned to the shipwrecked sailor.

"So, "Mr. Odysseus," if that's who you are, may I ask you a question?"

"Of course! Anything for a beautiful woman," he answered with a flourish. Maria smiled, which pissed Nick off. "When I call her that, I get 'the look.' When this asshole calls her beautiful, he gets a smile." Luckily, for once, he kept his thoughts as thoughts and didn't spit them out for everyone to hear.

"Why, for the love of the gods, did you have to shout out to the Cyclops to tell him who you were? He wound up killing your whole crew."

"How do you know about that?" the wanderer wondered.

Nick couldn't resist sticking his nose in: "She read about it. She has read just about everything that was ever written!"

"You mean someone wrote down what happened? About the war and the horse and my journey to find my way home?"

Maria nodded. "It's a very famous work; two—one about the Trojan War, one about your journey. But you didn't answer my question. You had all escaped and were safe, and then you couldn't resist yelling at your adversary. WHY?"

Odysseus shook his head in disgust. "You wanna know why I did that? You wanna know why? I'll tell you why. I can't keep my big mouth shut!!"

Maria just smiled, but Nick couldn't contain himself and burst into a fit of laughter, which the Greek from Ithaca did not take too kindly.

"It is not funny, my Greek koumbaro. I have been doing that my whole life, and it has caused me many problems."

Maria thought she'd better step in. "He's not laughing *at* you- -or even *with* you. HE'S LAUGHING AT HIMSELF. Nick has the biggest mouth I've ever seen, and he opens it at all the wrong times and says all the wrong things."

"And then he worries himself sick about it, right?" Odysseus asked.

"Night and day! Forever—," Nick added.

"You are like my brother," the famous Greek shouted as he grabbed Nick and hugged him again.

Maria had convinced herself that Nick wasn't gay, but she was starting to have her doubts about Odysseus. Suddenly, Nick let out a resounding "Whoa, back up a minute here!!"

"What is it, my fellow countryman?" Odysseus asked.

"Maria, are we supposed to believe that this character is *the* Odysseus, who came up with the Trojan Horse and took ten years to get home? Is that what he's selling?"

Maria looked at Ody, who nodded and put his hand on his heart. "But that would mean we've gone back over three thousand years.

"I guess so, Nick," Maria responded. "What other explanation could there be?"

This was upside down, Nick reasoned. He was the one who believed in all the fate stuff, that things happen for a reason, and that sometimes you had to suspend reality and just have faith. Maria was the skeptic. But she seemed to buy into Ody's story. Or was it that she was buying into Odysseus?

And then he remembered the visit from Aphrodite, which he thought was a dream. But what about the fact that there were no people or any sign indicating people were around somewhere? Oh, Lord, what was going on? How was he going to get to reality? Then he remembered his advice, which had worked the time he used it with Maria; maybe it would work with this guy, whoever the hell he was. He repeated it to himself three times: "Go soft, Nick, go soft, go soft."

He turned toward the warrior and asked as calmly and respectfully as possible: "Are you really Odysseus?"

"Yes, Nick, I am," Odysseus answered forthrightly.

"OK, then, that's good enough for me," Nick concluded. "That's good enough for me."

"I am glad that's settled," Ody proclaimed. "May I ask something of you before we proceed?"

The two-time travelers nodded. "Maria, your complexion tells me that your roots are somewhere in this beautiful part of the world, but the details of your face don't seem to be Greek. Am I correct?"

"Yes, you are. I am Sicilian, right here on this island."

"Ah, Sicilian. I should have known. In many ways, better than Greek."

"Man, this guy is smooth," Nick thought to himself. "Smooo....th!!" He had never seen Maria blush, but it looked like that was what she was doing. Holy shit! No wonder this Odysseus was one of the most famous men in the history of the world.

Zeus was about to slam a chunk of cheese into his mouth when Triandos pointed to the screen. That would have resulted in an uncharted flight off the mountain courtesy of the king's punting leg on a typical day. Still, these were exceptional circumstances, so Zeus swallowed his pride and the cheese and quickly turned his attention to the story unfolding before them.

"Both Maria and Nick have to make key decisions here, Father, so Vasilie just didn't want you to miss it," Aphrodite explained.

Whenever she called him "Father," he knew it was serious, so Zeus took back his silent pledge to beat the crap out of the wine man or, more accurately, gave himself a "rain check" for another day.

"—each of them had three hurdles to overcome, as it were. Nick has proven that he is honorable, wise, and a good guy - he showed that during my time as Maria during lunch duty. I told him how well he did when I was on the beach with him. So that's one run for him. Maria has changed Nick's life and made him more like the person he used to be or tried to be. One for her. They will each have to choose here in Sicily, which would be their second score. So, let's see how they do."

Maria suggested they go back to the blankets and decide what the best thing to do would be moving forward for Odysseus and themselves. Seemed reasonable. Maria was walking ahead of the two men, who were whispering.

"So, you and Maria--she tells me you are good friends, is that correct, koumbaro?" For some reason, it bothered Nick when Odysseus called him that, but since the ancient Greek was bigger, younger, and stronger, he thought discretion was called for - at least at first.

"Yes, we are very good friends.

"And you mean to say you have never wanted to…how do you put it…be something more than friends?"

"We are very good friends. Can we just let it go at that?"

"Yeah, but man, just look at her. What kind of a Greek are you?" Odysseus railed on. "What kind of Greek are you?"

Nick was getting tired of playing second fiddle to this guy, household name notwithstanding. First, Maria's apparent infatuation with him, smooth or not smooth - calls her beautiful and looking different from the Greeks. God knows what else he told her before Nick joined the conversation. Then this dismissive attitude...who the hell was he to question what kind of Greek Nick was. Nick was generally a pretty congenial guy, but when he lost it, it was never halfway. He stopped short and grabbed Odysseus by the shoulder and looked him square in the eyes, which was an accomplishment in and of itself since Nick was about a head shorter.

"Look, you relic from the past, it's not just what she looks like, although she is stunning and seductive, as you have discovered by opening your watery eyes. It's what she's like inside. She's perceptive and reflective and filled with passion and compassion, with a soul with no limit. And she has turned my life around. She taught me to look at the world differently, cherish the moment, think, to be who I am...no, to be better than who I am. I would not do anything to defame her for all the wealth or physical gratification in the world. You want to know what kind of Greek I am, lemme tell you: the kind who when he makes a promise to a woman, to *this* woman, he keeps it. That's the kind of Greek I am. As desirable as she is, I promised myself I would not let my feelings wander where they are not supposed to. And, figuratively, I have kept my word as hard as that has been. THAT'S THE KIND OF GREEK I AM. Do you have a problem with that?"

Odysseus' entire countenance changed, and he was beaming.

"Bravo, bravo!! Honor is a forgotten virtue, but you have shown the kind of Greek you are and the kind of man you are. You are my brother." The two Greeks hugged again as Maria turned around to see what was up.

"Oh, my God. Is the stereotype true? Let's go, you two lovebirds. It's getting dark."

As the "lovebirds" were making their way back toward Maria, Odysseus asked Nick provocative questions. "Niko, let me ask you something. I am bound and determined to get home to Ithaca, but it has been a long travail, and I may have to stay where I am for quite some time. Do you think Maria would stay here with me?"

This didn't take Nick by surprise as Ody thought it might. He *had*… often… kidded Maria that if Odysseus had met her instead of Calypso, he might never have left Sicily, and the run of history would have played out quite differently.

"Well, you'll have to ask *her* how she feels about it," was the quick answer.

"But how would *you* feel about it, Bro?"

Nick was impressed at how quickly Ody caught on to the modern vernacular. Well, he was very clever. "I love being with her very much, and I would miss her terribly. But if she wanted to *live The Odyssey* rather than just read about it—It would probably be her dream. You can tell her that whatever she decides is OK with me."

"You're a good man, Nick. A good man."

"Yeah, yeah, Ody. I try."

Odysseus walked over to Maria. They talked briefly, and then she came back toward Nick. She had a soft look on her face that Nick had never seen before and then broke into a warm smile.

"So, you're trying to dump me onto this ancient Greek, huh? Well, it's not gonna work, you sappy history teacher. You can't get rid of me that easily. Besides, who is gonna look out for you if I'm not there to keep you out of trouble?"

"Maria, you make me smile and laugh more than I deserve."

"Well, somebody has to," Maria replied with a big grin.

"Seriously, you are so sweet; thank you."

She gave him a hug and a quick kiss on the cheek. After turning three shades of red, Nick looked toward the spot where Odysseus had been standing, but he was gone. The beach, the ocean, the Mediterranean sky - all gone. He turned back toward Maria, wearing her "beige" outfit and getting ready to exit the cafeteria.

"Hey, Nick, you never told me how you liked Sicily."

"Huh?"

"Didn't you watch the video I gave you yesterday?"

"Oh, yeah, yeah. It was great, Maria."

"Oh, and here's the book I was talking about." She handed him a copy of *The Things They Carried*. "You'll like this: it's about Vietnam. Read it for tomorrow."

She winked at him as she was going out.

His friend would say that this whole day had too many moving parts. Nick's head was spinning with everything that had happened, and he decided to hurry and get the hell out of there before life threw him any more curves. But alas, he wasn't quick enough! One of his seniors was already two steps past Nick when he did a quick about-face and stopped short right in front of the beleaguered teacher. This kid was a good friend, but he was always busting Nick about something.

"Hey, Pappas, who have you been smooching with?"

"Bobby, not now. I'm not in the mood."

"Well, *she* must have been in the mood. You got a big lipstick mark on your left cheek. Hubba, hubba."

HOLY SHIT!

CHAPTER TWENTY-SEVEN
EXTRA INNINGS...

"Well, as they say, all's well that ends well. How about another round of desserts with some of that 'coffee' you've been brewing, Pythia. That would hit the spot." Zeus was ready to wrap things up.

"Your nose has never lost its knack for picking up the scent of things edible or drinkable, my dearest ruler of the universe. It would be good to break for coffee and something sweet, but we are not done, and neither is Maria or Nick."

Pythia had been relatively quiet during his whole affair. At first, her silence had been because Aphrodite and Triandos had essentially pulled the rug out from underneath her and Poseidon. But she did like a good mystery, and once she got over her snit, she decided to focus on what was happening to see if she could figure out where everything was headed. Normally, she would have given those assembled, chapter and verse, but she gave the floor to Aphrodite uncharacteristically. No one could remember her ever having been so gracious before. Poseidon felt she was acknowledging a good sleight of hand, and Hera thought she was trying to cover up her jealousy of Maria. Zeus just figured she was plastered.

Ever the polite goddess, Aphrodite started by thanking her hostess for the lovely get-together and bowed to the rest of those in attendance to allow her and Triandos to present their little charade. She then turned things over to her partner, who got right down to cases.

"Well, even though it looked like they're finished, the ball game's not over," Aphrodite's friend began. "We'll have to wait for the final score."

As stuffed and interested as he was, Zeus still could not tolerate this man, and the baseball metaphors were an annoying delay as far as he was concerned.

"Could we please get on with it?" he rumbled as more of an order than a question.

"Good point, your highness. To fulfill the prophecy, they had to perform three acts, with the third one being something very personal for the other person. So far, they have each done two, which leaves one more for each of them, so all three are completed. Are you with me so far?"

"It's not rocket science - whatever that means," Zeus threw in.

Triandos allowed himself an inward smile. He knew that if the king of gods understood, it was clear that everyone else did as well. And they did, but there was a question.

"After all this, I'm still not sure exactly what the 'prophecy' is. Did I miss something?" Hera asked.

Aphrodite jumped in: "To be honest, we're not quite sure. But it will be revealed once things have played out. Will that work for everyone?"

They all nodded. Zeus and Poseidon were pretty well gassed and would have agreed to just about anything. Still enamored with Maria, Apollo wanted to see as much more of her as he could. The goddesses took everything in stride, including the inebriated condition of the men, so a little more intrigue would be fascinating. Pythia? Well, she was in some ways similar to Maria: you could never exactly tell what she was thinking or what she would do!

CHAPTER TWENTY-EIGHT
THE RED DRESS

For once, Nick was looking forward to lunch duty. It wasn't as if he usually didn't like seeing his "Sicilian co-conspirator," as Maria wanted to call herself. Still, he often had the feeling that he would say or do something he would regret, and he usually did. Today, however, it seemed as if there wouldn't be any roadblocks to a smooth session. It was almost Christmas vacation, and he vowed to keep his opinions bottled up. Good plan, right? Well, that's what Nick thought. He got to the cafeteria before Maria did, which was fortunate because he was already sitting down when she walked in - had she been there first, he probably would not have been able to find his chair! And did she ever "walk-in!" She had on a red dress which she had not ever worn to school before - not solid red - sort of "speckled," which could only be described as electric. Well, many more descriptions zapped through his mind, including stunning, unbelievable, becoming, provocative…well, you get the idea. It was the last full day of school, which meant the last day of lunch duty. What a finish!

He was speechless, and then some. You could hardly blame him. There was Christmas right around the corner, which always put him in a tither. The students, despite their ages, were in their full holiday mode, which was fine but also added to the confusion. There were all his adventures, real, dreamed, or imagined, with all the gods. And now there was Maria, who wore a dress that was totally, well, just totally. Nick just sat there without saying a word for a good two minutes. When he finally got himself at least partially lucid, the only thing he could say was, "Not fair. Not fair, Maria!"

She laughed and smiled. She knew exactly what Nick was talking about. "So, I guess you like my dress, huh, Greek?"

Nick was still fumbling with his composure and trying to keep things under control. All he could say was, "Wow!" Of course, he repeated it about a dozen times but finally managed to rein himself in a bit. "Sorry, Maria. You look so beautiful in this."

"As opposed to my usual scrub woman ensemble every other day?"

"You know what I mean. Just a sincere compliment to a friend."

"Hey - just busting you. I appreciate it, even if you are drooling all over the table." They both laughed good-naturedly.

"Oh, Greek, I need to cover a class next period. OK, if I cut out a few minutes early?"

"Of course. If Brad comes by, I'll just tell him you won the lottery and resigned," Nick chided her. "Oh, and you said you liked the idea of letting the Vietnam day just go with the flow?"

"Yup, I think that would work well. We can do it the second day back after the break, OK?"

"Yeah, that's what I was thinking," Nick added. "Hey, listen, tomorrow is a half-day. I have some donuts and cider and candy canes and stuff--you wanna bring your 5th-period class down, and we'll just have a Christmas party? I mean, I don't want to override something you have planned."

"That sounds great. Maybe put on some music….and maybe you can play some music? Do you want my class to bring any food down?"

"Nah, I have plenty. Hey, not trying to get rid of you, but if you wanna go now to get settled in that class you're covering—"

"Oh, yeah, thanks." Maria got her stuff together, but as she was turning to leave, Nick signaled to her to come closer, which she did. He waved his hand along the length of her dress, smiled, and said the magic words: "HOLY SHIT," which produced a big smile on the face of his beautiful partner!

There were about eight minutes left in the lunch period, and it was like finding money for Nick. The kids were all relatively quiet; they were talking and happy but neither loud nor boisterous. He had no papers to correct; well, more precisely, he wasn't about to do any papers or any other work so close to Christmas. He wasn't even in the mood to work on his creative endeavors. So, his thoughts turned to Christmas, past, and present. As his best friend always said, Christmas does come faster with each passing year, and though he did his best to enjoy it and not get stressed, it was not an easy task. So, he took a break from all the "gotta get dones" and just thought about the Christmas party the next day with the combined history and English classes.

And, of course, this year, he had been re-introduced to thinking courtesy of his lunch duty partner. He was still in awe of how much she knew about everything, what other people (read "Nick") would be interested in, and how she was always at least a step ahead of both her students and her supposed equals - her colleagues. Never mind all the stuff with Sicily and the gods and the makeup of her soul. Then he had an inspiration, a "eureka" moment. Why try to figure out what was real and what was not? What was a dream, and what was a daydream? In his mind, one way or the other, so why not just accept things at face value, somewhat like the style of THE THINGS THEY CARRIED, which he read in one night! Yup, that was as good a plan as any. For once in his life, Nick was delighted with his decision. Now, back to something that was certainly not a dream...the red dress. Whew!

CHAPTER TWENTY-NINE
WHAT WILL BE, WILL BE...
OR WILL IT??

Well, here it was, the last day before Christmas vacation, the best school day of the year. Everyone was in a good mood, and a lighthearted feeling seemed to sparkle down the halls and bounce off the lockers and the lights. Each teacher had decorated the doors in the history wing to reflect Christmas in a particular decade. Nick had picked the 1940s, and his door was a nostalgic trip back in time. There were movie posters from *It's a Wonderful Life, The Best Years of Our Lives, Casablanca;* parts of the lead sheets from the songs "Have Yourself A Merry Little Christmas," "White Christmas," "I'll Be Home For Christmas;" catalog pictures of trains, dolls, and other toys from that era; and several headlines from major events of WWII. The door *was* Nick, a comment Maria made on her way in with her class. "Thanks," was all he said. She didn't reply, but her eyes doubled in size to reflect her surprise at the brevity of his response.

The room was decorated in every conceivable way. There was a handmade wooden fireplace replica with stockings, lights, and a garland. In the far corner, there was a tree, complete with ornaments, strings of beads, lights, and candy canes, with a dozen or so neatly wrapped presents at its base. And the rest of the room looked like something out of a Christmas catalog. A table filled with things to eat and drink and Christmas songs resonated through the air.

"All this for my class, Greek?"

"Just for you, Maria," Nick laughed.

A picture caught Maria's eye on the way past Nick's desk. It was of him, his buddy Anthony, and their dog Susie - taken in Vietnam. She picked it up to look at it closely, which she did for quite a while.

"Nice picture, Nick," she commented sincerely. It was one of the few of himself that he liked, and he thanked her. He was in his early twenties and had a dark mustache and thick black hair to spare. This was too easy for Maria, who felt she owed him at least a couple of good-natured ribbings.

"Wow, Nick. Look at all that hair! Looks great! What happened to it? Come on, was that really you?"

The gods were watching as well. They had gathered for what was hopefully the last leg in this odyssey. The year 2020 was arriving in about ten days, and whether that was part of the equation or not, they didn't want to miss what might happen on December 23, just in case things settled in this calendar year.

Zeus was impressed after viewing the picture: "So, this guy was a soldier. Good for him. Good for him!"

"I told you he was OK, dad," Aphrodite reminded Zeus. "And you don't need me to tell you about Maria. Just look—"

"Yeah, I know. Just look at her. Wow!" Apollo interjected.

"Yeah, just look!" Zeus echoed.

Aphrodite scowled and vigorously shook her head.

"You two are idiots - overaged adolescents. WHAT I MEANT WAS; just look at what she's done to Nick...how she's changed him in only a few months."

"Well, that's what we meant, too, right Pop?" Apollo countered.

"Yes, certainly. You didn't let us finish!" Zeus added.

"Yeah, right," Athena threw in.

Poseidon, of all "people," saved the day and kept this from possibly going further than it had to. "Dite, how about grabbing us some of their treats. They have an overabundance of good stuff, and I'm sure they wouldn't mind sharing with us. Especially if they didn't know about it. It's always better to think on a full stomach."

"Good idea Unc. I'll see what I can do. Be right back. Try to keep your emotions under control while I'm gone." Aphrodite was off in a flash.

Meanwhile, Maria and Nick headed to the refreshment table themselves. On their way, they were exchanging pleasantries with the students, who were busy giving gifts, opening up plates of cookies they had brought, and quaffing some apple cider.

"Pretty good spread, Nick. Got any Italian cookies?" Maria asked, smiling. Nick was smiling since he had gotten some just in case she wanted any.

"Here you go, Maria. For my favorite Sicilian." He was laughing as he handed her a package of Stella Doro cookies. "Are these OK?"

"Well, I haven't tasted them yet!" she deadpanned.

They went back and forth lightheartedly and could barely control their laughter. Neither could many of the students who stopped to watch.

Maria threw her head back with the clincher. "We're like an old married couple!"

Somehow Nick managed to stay connected to the goings-on about him and reflect internally on that premise. Obviously, Maria was kidding, but it still caught his attention. Of course, that would have to have been in a different lifetime, but he couldn't help but wonder what it might have been like. Probably a couple of rounds every day slugging it out…but they still would have been some combination. His trip to never, never land was interrupted by a student's thirsty plea.

"Hey, Mr. Pappas, do you have any more cider? This container is almost drained."

"Huh? Oh, sure, there are at least three more gallons under the table. Help yourself."

It was then that Nick noticed a young, beautiful woman in his room. She introduced herself as the substitute for one of the science teachers and asked if she could take some food for her class.

"Of course, there's plenty," Nick responded. Which she did - take plenty. There was something familiar about her, but he couldn't quite place where he had seen her before. Something about her, though.

It might have pleased Nick to know that the gods enjoyed his largess, especially the king, who was in love with the donut holes he gobbled down. Meanwhile, one of the kids asked Nick if he would play something on his keyboard. He obliged with several Christmas songs and some Broadway tunes as well.

"Not bad, Pappas," one of his longtime students cracked.

"I concur, Nick. Very nice," Maria added.

"Thanks very much," was Nick's reply. Simple and sincere.

While enjoying the cookies and cider, the gods had not lost sight of the fact that something was supposed to happen to put this whole thing to rest. The class period was winding down, and nothing out of the ordinary seemed imminent. Everyone turned to look at Pythia, who was busy enjoying a giant candy cane.

It was Apollo who spoke up first, with his usual simplicity.

"Well?"

"Well, what?" came the reply from the Oracle as she ran her tongue up and down the cane.

"Wow, that looks good," Zeus commented.

All eyes turned toward the king, and Pythia gave him a big wink. The whole group broke into one big belly laugh.

Zeus, as usual, was a few steps behind. "What?" was his out-of-touch question, which he repeated several times. He and Nick had a lot in common when it came to grasping what was going on at any given moment. "What's so funny? What—" and then he got it. Normally he would have blown his stack, but he seemed to have caught the Christmas spirit - quite a feat considering the origin of Christmas was technically still about a thousand years in the future. "OK, OK, I get it. The king is the joker again."

Hera could only smile and reward her husband with a big kiss. "I'm proud of you for keeping your composure, dear." She then turned to the Oracle.

"Well, 'cuz,' what's up?"

"Be patient. The class is not finished. Remember, 'It's not over till the fat lady sings.' Something can still happen. There are still a few minutes left.'" By now, the gods had become reasonably well versed in "modern" figures of speech, and, though they hadn't heard this particular one before, they got the drift. Even Zeus! So - they turned their attention back to the party.

Maria had been carrying around a small, plain, brown shopping bag. She and Nick were standing near the tree as she handed it to him. "Here you go, Nick, Merry Christmas!" Four words were written on the outside: "To Nick, the Greek."

"Thanks, Maria, Nick said warmly. I have something for you, too."

He reached under the tree, grabbed a small wrapped box, and handed it to his guest.

"Thanks, Nick. Hey, this is light as a feather. Is that what you got me? A feather?"

Just at that moment, the bell rang, signaling the end of class. The students gathered their stuff; most stopped to wish the two teachers a Merry Christmas.

Zeus was like a little kid at - well - Christmas.

"What did they get each other? Aren't they going to open their presents? I wanna see what they got."

"Keep your shirt on, big guy," Pythia commanded, but not in her usual contemptuous fashion. "Watch—"

"Nick, is it all right if I wait till Christmas to open this?" Maria wondered.

"Sure. On one condition," Nick answered with a big smile. "That you seriously consider writing that book about teaching with me."

"You drive a hard bargain, Pappas. That sounds like a good idea."

"Great, Maria. We're gonna be a good team! Do you wanna know what your gift is?"

"I'd rather be surprised. But maybe you could look in the bag I brought--?"

"Yes, dear," Nick replied, still grinning like a homesick possum.

Watching from above, or wherever they were, the gods reacted, typically, by gender. The Oracle, Hera, Athena, and Aphrodite smiled knowingly, while the "guys" seemed more puzzled than ever. Athena decided to lay it all out to avoid any misunderstandings.

"May I," she requested cordially. "You can stop me if I take any missteps, Pyth. Will that work?"

"Fine with me," answered the Oracle, who was by now face deep in Christmas cookies.

"It's pretty simple. Each of our two players needed to perform three acts - the third one privately and unselfishly - to keep things on an even course and fulfill the prophecy. Each of them gave a personal Christmas present to the other, and each of the gifts was poignant and thoughtful. And, they will work together on a book...well, they *think* that's all there is to it."

"Never mind all this prophecy, save the universe stuff - we can get to that in a minute. But first, I wanna know what their presents to each other were," Zeus grumbled.

"Well, Nick is about to open his...take a look," Athena instructed.

Nick was, indeed, about to look at his present. It was a book. But not just an ordinary book: it was about a father and son who retrace the travels of Odysseus. He read the inscription:

"It certainly has been an odyssey...maybe it's the Greek in you
Looking forward to our next journey...Your Sicilian cafeteria

accomplice…Maria

It was very apparent that Nick was touched. He tried to think of something profound to say, but, luckily, all he could come up with was: "Thanks so much, Maria."

"Enjoy," she smiled in return.

"But what did he give *her*?" Zeus persisted.

Hera nodded at Aphrodite as she said. "You'd better tell him, or we'll be here till Eternity."

"He wrote a song for her. And I can't let you see the whole thing, but I'll tell you the first line cause I think it captures Maria very well."

Zeus was floored. "This guy wrote a song? Are you serious?"

Aphrodite was losing her patience and was also hungry, and she wanted to get some food before it was gone. "Do you want to hear it or not, Dad?"

Zeus nodded apologetically. "What is it?"

"Inscrutable, but beautiful is she…."

"Wow, that's a great first line!" Zeus remarked. "Ah, but, uh, what does 'inscrutable' mean?" Everyone cracked up as Hera handed the king a cup of apple cider.

"Here, dear. Be a good boy, and let's see how this turns out."

The king took the cider, but he wasn't entirely done. "I'm pulling rank here," he proclaimed in a very stately manner.

{Whoever is reading this: did you ever experience something that seemed to be happening in slow motion? Or where time itself abruptly came to a standstill? Psychologists and physicists will give you cerebral explanations, but perhaps it was something simpler. Maybe it was the gods taking a hand. Read on….}

The scene in Nick's room turned slowly into still life as he and Maria became portraits of themselves, almost like Oscar Wilde's *The Picture Of Dorian Gray.*

"You didn't?" Pythia asked fearfully. "You know that you have a tiny window of moments, or else the whole-time mechanism will be thrown asunder."

"I DID," Zeus retorted. "And, if someone will just answer one question, I'll start things back up again. Pardon my language, but what the HELL was the prophecy."

Athena smiled. "I got this. As I was saying, each of them did the three things they needed to do, culminating today. Prophecies do not stop, not any of them, and not this one. The decision Maria made back in Sicily kept history running as it should, but prophecies are also about individuals, their lives, and their effect on each other. Maria made Nick into a better human being in so many aspects of his persona, and he was there to allow her to have that impact on someone's life. Now, they will be working together. Got it, Dad?"

Remarkably, Zeus had gotten it. He snapped his finger, and things were set in motion once again...

Maria stopped to take a candy cane while Nick was ruminating about the Sicilian Odyssey they had been on. He held the book tightly while he watched her leave. As she walked out the door, she turned and gave him the most magical smile Nick had ever seen. No one, not even the gods, could predict what would happen in the future, but there was one thing for certain - he would never forget that moment and that smile.

EPILOGUE

*there are no coincidences –
everything happens for a reason.*

CPSIA information can be obtained
at www.ICGtesting.com
Printed in the USA
LVHW090230060922
727610LV00017B/1147

9 780998 300764